CW01217190

Contents

Part One

Part Two

Part Three

Part Four

Part Five

Part Six

PART ONE

Black Pudding Land

If you go and visit Black Pudding Land,
You'll find very quickly life is grand,
Each person you meet is soon your friend,
Best wishes to you each one will send.
You will always find a friendly smile
As you walk a yard or walk a mile,

Any trouble you have, you can share,
Because for you, support is always there,
To offer a warm and helping hand,
Assist you on your feet to stand.
You will not be left alone,
To struggle along all on your own

It's a land that exists so far away,
Where children all can safely play,
Where no danger lurks to cause them harm.
Each child is safe, each child is calm.
Black Pudding soldiers march around,
Patrolling each section of the ground,

The Chief Black Pudding rules with even hand,
Ensuring peace throughout the land,
And his riches all of his subjects they share.
They trust the chief and know he is fair.
Nobody owns or has any more,
Than any of the Puddings gone before.

So, come journey now please come with me,
Where people are forever free,
All worries just leave them far behind.
Expand imagination in your mind.
Put aside your woes and earthly care,
And in merriment with me please share.

When you've experienced its' peace and joy,
The laughter of each girl and boy.
Compassion you will find all around
As you tread your feet across the ground.
With all the friendship close at hand,
You'll not want to leave Black Pudding Land.

Celebration

The daytime light was sleeping
And the nights dark roamed the sky,
Black Pudding land it was quiet
As the passing hours went slowly by.

Then at once a very loud tapping
Disturbed the peace that each pudding enjoyed.
Black Pudding soldiers stirred awake,
Each one of them quite annoyed.

The young Heinz Beans went crying
To the parents still asleep,
Waking them forcefully out of slumbers
So comfortable, warm and deep.

“What is that noise they cried out?
It's making us feel so scared.
We’ve never stopped our shaking
From the very first time we heard”.

They listened at the window,
Trying to see what the noise could be?
But an unknown fear engulfed them,
They became much too scared to see.

Sitting quietly around the table,
On chairs made from freshly gathered straw,
Then each one of them was startled
By a knock upon their door.

“Who is it?” Loudly shouted father,
In an unnaturally high-pitched voice,
“It’s me your next-door neighbour,
Come on out we must all rejoice.

I've heard from the Chief Black Pudding,
We all must go down into the square.
He has some great news to tell us,
Glad tidings we all must share".

Their door they quickly opened
Walked together slowly down the stairs,
And greeted by chocolate celebrations
Having a conference with two green pears.

"Have you heard? We've all been discussing
What this exciting news could be,
Let's hurry let's join the others,
We've brought torches to help us see".

So quickly all put their coats on,
Scrambled and gathered in the square
Where they saw the Chief Black Pudding
With his armed guards all standing there.

A smile gleamed on all their faces
As they stood still with sparking eyes,
Then a rumour started spreading,
They had captured two of the Lard's spies.

The last months many suspicions
Which had spread much panic around.
Who exactly was stealing secrets,
Soldiers had their ears close to the ground.

No one had trusted anybody,
Each person lived their lives in fear
That the traitor stealing the secrets,
Was somebody that they held dear.

But tonight, suspicion was lifted,
Each Pudding knew deep in their hearts
It was now time to breathe out more freely,
Drink, dance, carouse with Royal Jam Tarts.

Then the Chief Pudding hoisted high his banner,
Silence crept slowly amongst the crowd.
They knew they should be silent,
As the king spoke in a voice so loud.

"My fellow Puddings, listen closely
To everything I have to say,
We've stopped the secrets being stolen
Being slyly whisked away.

It is down to these brave soldiers,
The ones standing here next to me
That each citizen can truly believe,
Black Pudding Land remains free.

Not considering the danger
In the task that they had at hand,
They only had the thought of saving
Our beloved Black Pudding Land.

They captured two of the Lards robbers
While they were searching behind a wall.
And a soldier overheard a noise
Which turned out to be Lard's secret call.

Curious as to what the noise was,
They went down to investigate.
And they caught both of them red handed
Trying to escape through the main gate.

Hidden deep inside their pouches,
Were the plans of our defence,
Which had helped us to live safely
Stopping us all from feeling tense.

If they'd fallen into the Lards hands,
We'd have a big fight on our hands,
But thanks to these brave Pudding soldiers
We have peace reigning in our lands".

So that day each Black Pudding soldier
Receiving thanks for completing their deed,
Were then carried high to the town hall
And given drink and food on which to feed.

From that day the Black Pudding people,
Realised they all should again learn to trust
Each person who once they had doubted
Repairing that which once had been bust.

So together they all became stronger,
Their society, once more was at peace.
But aware that the Lard he was stalking,
And his attacks one day may increase.

Alert to the threats in the future,
The Chief made sure that all larders were stocked.
With food, refreshments and weapons,
And the doors could be quickly unlocked.

The Dream of The Chief Black Pudding

Version one

The Chief Black Pudding Soldier
Went to bed one night quite tired,
He'd had trouble with his cabinet,
And more than one of whom he'd fired.

They had no imagination,
They were complacent with their power.
He had called a cabinet meeting,
To be convened within the hour.

Things were said, not much was friendly.
The Chief then yelled "I've had enough".
He said, "I'm going to make some changes,
And if you don't like them all, well tough".

He banged the table with his standard,
It was pure luck it did not bend,
And all those whom he had fired,
To the gravy mines he did send.

After that he adjourned the meeting,
And put his crown back on his head.
He told them all that he was tired
And he was going off to bed.

There with his head upon his pillow,
His mind it soon began to dream,
With images drifting to and fro,
Just like a swirling bubbling stream.

All his fears about his people,
The listless life they now did lead,
And the order he'd created,
These his thoughts began to feed.

He dreamt a darkened mass existed,
And all the Puddings cared not less.
They just did not seem to worry,
About creating such a mess.

Good fun with games and socials,
Filled up all their empty lives,
The only things that had a purpose,
Were bees filling up their hives.

No cares in Pudding Land, all happy.
Every day the sun will shine.
What Puddings wanted, they just snatched at,
The operative word was "mine".

But a dark mass it was spreading,
Cross the sky beneath the clouds.
It was not seen or even noticed,
By the self-indulgent crowds.

They awoke one day in darkness,
Waiting for the sun to rise,
The Puddings could not believe it,
The darkness had filled the skies.

All the streets soon filled with panic.
And a deafening frightening sound.
There was shouting, yelling, screaming,
There was scurrying all around.

Like rats which ran through sewers,
No-one knew which way to go.
Some were falling down and crawling
Oh, how they panicked so.

No electric worked their light bulbs,
No lifts went up and down.
No bright lights illumed the trade signs
In shops all around the town.

The life they'd known had changed now,
Their pointless fun had come to an end.
The town committee held a meeting,
And a message they decreed to send.

All Puddings should end their panic,
Panicking would only cause pain.
They must all pull themselves together,
And start working together again.

The Puddings gradually took notice,
Accepted, they lived now in the dark,
They cleaned and fixed their homes up.
Sausages returned to clean up the park.

They all found that when they were working,
Satisfaction soon quickly returned,
It was a feeling they'd forgotten,
Something for all their souls had yearned.

Soon work and play they were balanced,
All Black Puddings as one they did see.
If they lived life in moderation,
How contented each Pudding would be.

On waking, the Chief put his clothes on,
And to the cabinet room quickly returned,
Reconvening the suspended meeting,
To discuss all of the things, he had learned.

The Pudding members entered slowly,
Cereal bowls were held in their hands,
As the Chief Pudding proclaimed his message,
To be preached throughout all the lands.

"Our Puddings' lives, they have no meaning,
They drift around each day like straw,
They're filled with dissatisfaction,
But they won't feel that anymore.

I am going to form an army,
Our enemies are watching all around,
Namely Lard who lives o'er the border,
And yearly takes more of our ground".

The ministers in full agreement,
Went into the squares to spread the word.
To share with all Black Puddings
The Chiefs' wise words they all had heard.

All Black Puddings then found they has a purpose,
Soldiers stood proudly in many ranks.
Soon they held a big celebration,
To give the Chief Black Pudding all their thanks.

They were glad that they had a leader,
Who cared so much for their needs.
And they all knew in trust they'll follow,
Wherever their Chief Black Pudding leads.

They partied and sang in the town square,
Until the darkness it slowly did creep
And the Puddings back home they all drifted,
It was time for them all to sleep.

The Chief's Christmas Dinner

It was Christmas day in Black Pudding town,
Snow was lying all over the ground.
The air was filled with children's laughter,
There was merriment everywhere to be found.

Fried eggs were playing on skateboards,
They raced with poached eggs and scrambled.
Burgers played with their sausage meat fritters
Black Pudding soldiers on duty just ambled.

The Chief Black Pudding was feeling quite festive
He ordered a meal to be set for his friends.
Food was laid in the middle of the table,
And the drinks were spread out at both ends.

There were buns, and cream and a large sponge cake.
The biggest they'd ever seen yet.
But a young Black Pudding soldier, got greedy,
He just ate, and he ate, and he ate.

People stopped talking and just sat there looking
At him, and some were really quite shocked.
No one was surprised, that while he was eating,
The greedy young soldier's jaw locked.

He started to cry and his body was shaking.
His last cake fell out from his hand.
The Chief Black Pudding retorted,
"You're the greediest soldier in the land".

A Black Pudding doctor was present,
And prescribed his jaw would soon be released,
But as a punishment passed down by the Chief,
The poor soldier could not leave the feast.

It was painful for him to be watching,
Whilst sitting upright on his stool,
But an opinion gradually dawned on him,
That he had been such a greedy young fool.

If he'd just ate his food in moderation,
The festivities he'd be able to join in.
He wanted to turn back the clock,
To when the Chiefs' party once more did begin.

But he can't, so he just sits solemnly waiting,
For his jaw to be slowly released,
Unfortunately, the longer the time it was taking,
His embarrassment was greatly increased.

Soldiers laughed and pointed their fingers,
They had no sympathy at all for their friend,
Then as suddenly as it seized, his jaw released,
The soldiers' torture was now at an end

The festivities went on and continued,
Into the very early hours towards dawn.
Then people gasped thinking it had happened again,
But the soldier this time he did yawn.

Loud laughter was raised to the rafters,
As soldiers watched, and shook their weary heads,
And they all talked about what had just happened,
As they fell sleepily into their beds.

This tale is told to young Black Puddings,
To help them to learn from the soldiers' daft deed,
It is better to eat food in moderation,
And not to give in to their insatiable greed.

Princess Kathleen

Just who was in that black car,
Which drove past the wondering crowd.
They'd been standing and watching for hours
Their conversations animated and loud.

The headlines so large in the paper
Said a young lady would visit that day,
Wanting to talk to all the Black Puddings,
She had so much that she wanted to say.

No more details at all had been printed,
No clues of the lady revealed.
The lady's mysterious identity,
To all had been deeply concealed.

All of the Black Puddings had gathered
And watched as the car slowly went by.
No-one stirred when a frying egg saucer
Made a flight travelling fast in the sky.

So who is this mysterious lady?
What words are she wanting to say?
Is she somebody who once had lived here,
Then left and went travelling away?

Necks craned to look in through the windows,
But each glass was tinted dark black,
Only a shadowy mysterious figure
Was seen seated alone in the back.

A strange eerie silence was spreading,
Muffling out the incessant noise,
Only screeches and impatient shouting,
Came from Walls Sausages, young girls & boys.

All parents tried their best to comfort,
As the car halted by steps near the hall
The Chief Black Pudding soldier was waiting,
She was pleased he had answered her call.

The puddings as one all pushed forward
When the door it became gradually ajar
And the mysterious, but lovely young lady
Started walking slowly, away from the car.

She was such a beautiful Black Pudding,
Like a princess and all dressed in black,
Her hair it was black and was flowing,
Coming to rest half way, down her smooth back.

The crowd motionless stood there in silence
Watching her as she was making her way,
To where the Chief Pudding was standing,
Now an old man, with hair turning grey.

Smiling, he walked over to meet her,
Opened arms which were strong and so wide,
She ran the last steps up to reach him,
Fell into his arms and in happiness cried.

Then the crowd they all began to murmur,
After witnessing the developing scene,
Then they realised at once what her name was,
It was his daughter, the young Princess Kathleen.

They all cheered, waved their arms and all chanted,
Calling her name with such joy loud and clear,
She turned to face all the Black Puddings,
Her friends and family, who she loved so dear.

"My friends thank you all for your warm welcome,
It truly enlivens my heart,
I have so much that I want to tell you,
I really don't know where to start"

Then the Black Pudding soldiers grew silent,
They hung on each kind, spoken sweet word.
This Princess Kathleen was their favourite,
And for whom each one of them cared.

She had grown up surrounded by riches,
But she spent so much time with the poor.
She helped those who could join the army,
To protect Puddings if Lard came to war.

But now she was standing all grown up,
They embraced every word that she said.
Then a gasp of surprise was emitted
When she announced, that she was to be wed.

The Chief Pudding just stared quite astounded.
So surprised at the words that he'd heard.
His Princess he'd spent his life loving,
Was announcing she was to be paired.

As she walked to her father still smiling,
A tear slowly escaped from her eye.
She went to him, and held him quite tightly,
Said she loved him and gave a deep sigh.

She turned to the Puddings still waiting,
For her to explain, what did it all mean?
Had she given up all chance of her ruling?
Was she never one day to be queen?

"Black Pudding soldiers, hear me please, please listen,
Sacrifices sometimes must be made.
We have always been looking for helpers,
But so many times we have all been betrayed.

Today I announce an alignment,
One which should make each of your hearts sing.
I have accepted a proposal of marriage
From his highness the great Burger King.

He has promised he'll be there to help us
If again we are under attack.
He would never fail once to support us,
We'd always find that he'd have our back.

When time comes and it's my turn to govern,
Our two countries they would become one.
No interference in our way of living,
And all fear of the Lard would be gone.

Of course, this is just a proposal,
To our Chiefs' answer I'll loyally defer.
I have only the best of intentions,
For you Puddings for whom I truly care".

The Chief opened his arms and walked forward,
Took hold of her nervous gloved hand.
"In my daughter I have belief in,
And to all Puddings I make this command.

All Puddings will gather and welcome,
Our Princess Kathleen's groom to be.
When he visits our Black Pudding kingdom,
Exhibiting happiness for all to see.

Kathleen has decided to love him,
She was never coerced by his force.
I will welcome him into our family,
Making merry and drinking much sauce".

Preparations were made by the soldiers,
Ensuring all decorations looked right,
And when the Burger King made his appearance,
They cheered and partied deep into the night.

Here started the Puddings' allegiance
With the Burger King and his crisp fries,
And when the Princess and the Burger King married,
Tears of happiness flowed from all of their eyes.

Black Pudding soldiers and their Burger comrades,
Formed an army by all to be feared.
And any doubt still left remaining,
Over time, all gradually were cleared.

The Brides Dance

A strange day dawned in Black Pudding Town,
There were no single men to be seen.
The Chief Black Pudding scratched his head
As he stood bemused next to his queen.

Then he realised what the date was
And a smile crept over his face.
He knew they'd return the very next day,
But for now, they were in a safe place.

The young lady Puddings ran frantic,
Today would be their only chance
To find themselves a husband,
To accompany them to the brides dance.

They spent all day looking high and low,
There was no crevice in which they didn't look.
And then one bright girl found inspiration,
Turning on the oven, she started to cook.

As the meal was prepared the fragrance did drift
To the hills where the men had all gone.
Very soon they all were defeated
Slowly they drifted, returned one by one.

As they entered the gates they were ambushed,
"Marry me" was each girls doleful cry,
One by one the men all relented,
With a smile and a resigning deep sigh.

Some of the girls were so happy to have partners,
To accompany them to the bride's dance,
But others missed out and they were lonely
Knowing they had missed out on their chance.

They'd be prepared the next time and be ready,
Determined they'd not again shed a tear,
And until then they would practice their dancing,
While preparing for the next coming leap year.

Sports Day

Sports day came in Black Pudding town,
All the citizens had gathered there,
There were shots to put, races to run,
And lots of high fences to clear.

The stadium had filled from bottom to top
With Bacon, Sausage and Eggs,
And little Black Pudding Soldiers
Who were exercising, strengthening their legs.

They know one day, it will be their turn,
To compete along with their brave dads,
But that day was such a long way off
They were still, only tiny wee lads.

Contestants entered and the crowd stood and cheered,
Hats and scarfs were flown high into the air,
Everybody there that day was so happy,
There was no one, who harboured a care.

On your marks, get set, go. The pistol was fired,
It made such a very loud noise,
Everybody knew the gun wasn't real,
It was just, one of a young soldiers' toys.

But was it? A bird from the sky came tumbling,
It fell and landed right there at the feet
Of a runner, who promptly retrieved it,
Lo and behold, it was very dead meat.

The starter was late and he really was rushing,
Had not picked up the safe starting gun,
He'd picked up his own hunting pistol,
Not the one that belonged to his son.

Poor starter, a Walls prime beef burger,
Was feeling embarrassed and very deep fried,
So embarrassed was he at his deadly mistake,
He just cried, and he cried, and he cried.

Some soldiers they came, trying to comfort,
It took them all very nearly an hour,
Until he was able to start again the first race
It was four times around the Black Tower.

The race it was close, then it came to an end
And the winner received his reward,
He was touched on both of his shoulders,
By the Chief Black Pudding's jewelled sword.

Everybody there enjoyed a good time,
Wishing the day would just go on and on.
But they soon were dismayed, as the clock face displayed,
The time of the games was near gone.

When the events of the day finally ended,
And the champion Black Pudding was found.
He was raised up on strong Pudding shoulders,
And loud cheers went all the way round.

He was carried to the proud Chief Black Pudding,
And was placed on a seat by his side.
Both in the regal, royal carriage,
They waved, as they went for a ride.

The town's champion, he was celebrated,
He'd be honoured throughout the next year,
Or until he tripped and hurt himself,
And the pain caused him to shed a tear.

All the Sausages they had their duties,
To make sure the grounds they were clean,
The Eggs stretched their legs as they undid the pegs,
Removing a tent from where it had been.

All children had gone home excited,
And climbed reluctantly into their beds,
The events of the day, just would not go away,
They kept on spinning around in their heads.

The Black Pudding Soldiers, reassembled,
They had to continue to practice so hard,
There was always a threat of a long, long war,
With their distasteful, thick, enemy, Lard.

Soon the events of the day, they all faded.
Normality it crept forward and on,
Until the countdown told all of the Puddings,
Another twelve months had all gone.

Preparations again they were started,
And all the Puddings they would soon all begin
To strive for their own peak of fitness,
For the honour that is again there to win.

The Black Pudding War

Each day the brave Black Pudding soldiers,
Practiced and trained really hard,
Readying themselves to repel an attack
From their old dreaded enemy.... Lard.

The last time an attack came was
When the Puddings were all fast asleep.
Until awoken by the screams and the shouting,
As the wrath of the Lard it did sweep.

Lard came sliding in down from the mountains,
Covering every square inch of the ground.
When puddings looked out of their windows,
The pulsating Lard was all around.

When it happened, their Chief had the answer,
A weapon was hidden away in his store.
Designed to protect all of his subjects,
And put an end to their fear of war.

The soldiers were sent to the storeroom,
And were told to prepare their defence,
And when they saw all the bags that were stored there,
They knew their Chief Pudding spoke sense.

The soldiers when they were all ready,
Sprayed into the air unsifted white flour.
The flour spread engulfing the lard and,
The battle was won in the hour.

Then the vanquished Lard was taken prisoner,
And into the deep, damp, dark cells he was thrown.
To gaze on all the Pudding celebrations,
Defeated, and dreaming of home.

The next day the Chief Black Pudding soldier,
Sat in judgement against the Lard,
Sentencing him to 10 years in their prison,
Where he'd grow solid, and so very hard.

The soldiers locked away all their weapons,
And continued with their peace-time job,
Teaching each young pork sausage,
How it is wrong if they all steal and rob.

But soon from inside the cell's darkness,
A loud scrapping sound they all heard,
When the guard went and did his inspection,
The Lard, had completely disappeared.

The soldiers immediately went hunting,
But these the Lard he managed to evade,
Now, he's back in the hills where he came from,
To plan for the next time he'd invade.
That's why all the Black Pudding soldiers
Train hard and practice each day.
So, the next time the Lard approaches,
They will again quickly drive him away.

The Chiefs Birthday

The streets were full of people,
They were shouting, cheering loud.
There was not one morbid person,
In the thronging, singing crowd.

They were marching to a party,
Which was going to last all day,
This was no time for work or rest,
It was only time to play.

The drink was flowing freely,
Food was catered for each need,
With plates piled high they took their places,
And with relish began to feed.

Some guests gasped in amazement,
At the silver knives and forks.
Intrigued at all the detail,
On the dish that held used corks.

Troubles were all soon forgotten,
As the people joined in play.
And medals that were achieved in war,
Hung proudly on display.

A toast was raised to wish him health,
The Chief smiled and took a bow.
But as he bowed they heard a click,
Then he tried to rise, but, “Ow!”

His senior aid, he lent a hand,
To try hard to get him straight,
As pressure was put upon his back,
The Chief cried out aloud, "No! Wait!"

No-one it seemed could help him,
Standing there with his back bent.
There then arrived a Doctor Egg,
The one for whom his wife had sent.

"Please take it easy, will you Chief,
I'll quickly sort the problem out.
You'll soon be dancing with the rest,
Of that fact please have no doubt".

These were the words the Doctor spoke,
As he stood behind the Chief,
He promised him he would be straight,
And he would soon have such relief.

He lay the Chief down on his back,
His feet pointing in the air.
He asked someone to hold him down.
Then climbed high upon a chair.

He stood above the Chiefs' crowned head,
Arms swinging to and fro.
Then looking closely at the feet,
Towards them he did quickly go.

He flew and landed with his hands
Tight around the Chiefs' golden shoes,
Then pulled them down as he hit the ground,
It was the best cure he could choose.

A piercing yell then filled the air,
But soon the Chief he again gave a smile.
As relief crept through and filled his bones,
And he lay there for quite a while.

Sure, he was feeling alright,
And he was confident he could rise.
The time was right to join the dance,
And give his subjects a big surprise.

So up he jumped right off the ground,
As one the Puddings gave a gasp.
And a helping hand came quickly out,
For the Chief Pudding Soldier to grasp.

Standing upright, he rubbed his back,
He turned to Doctor Egg to say,
How glad he was that he came around,
Managing to save the day.

Modestly Dr Egg, bowed his head,
Then a Soldier standing near,
Was asked if would he kindly take him,
To make sure he's filled with cheer.

Dr. Egg walked up to the position,
That was especially for him prepared,
And the cheers of the crowd slowly died down,
As the food they gladly all shared.

The day wore on, and night drew in,
People began drifting away.
Discussing as they went along,
The happenings of the day.

Now all is quiet and all at peace,
Puddings lay their weary heads.
All dreaming dreams of lovely things,
Wrapped warm and snug inside their beds.

The Dream of The Chief Black Pudding
Version two

A darkened mass existed,
And the Puddings cared not less,
They never once did worry,
Their world was in a mess.

Just fun and games and socials,
Filled up their busy lives,
Like bees producing honey,
And filling up their hives.

No care in the world, they're happy,
Every day the sun will shine,
What they wanted, they just snatched at,
And the operative word was, mine.

But one day, a strange thing happened,
The sun it did not rise,
No Pudding could believe it,
No sunlight bathed their eyes.

They ran through streets in panic,
Each uttering horrific sound,
Screaming, shouting, yelling,
Scurrying all around.

Like rats living in sewers,
Each Pudding grasped at straws,
Some falling down and crawling,
Like animals on all fours.

No electric for their light bulbs,
No lifts went up or down,
No lights illuming trade signs,
In shops around the town.

The life they knew was finished,
Fun and games came to an end.
The Chief Black Pudding held a meeting,
He a message to all, did send.

He asked the Puddings to stop their moaning,
Gather up their strength and then
Just pull themselves together,
And start working again.

So, the Puddings pulled together,
Began working in the dark,
They cleaned and fixed their homes up,
Young Eggs cleaned up the park.

Eventually they realised,
Satisfaction did exist,
Then the Puddings all discovered,
It was something they had missed.

If work and play was balanced,
The Puddings began to see,
When doing things in moderation,
How much happier they would be.

Pudding scientists, they worked daily,
A solution they tried to find
To reverse the situation,
It stretched the cleverest mind.

Then one day a shout of triumph
Came from the laboratory in the hall,
Of the Pudding high school college,
They ran to share the news with all.

Firstly, to the Chief Black Pudding,
They explained all they had found,
It was the Lard who had spread poison,
Scattering it over their ground.

A darkened mist then rose up
Rising up so very high,
It slowly spread and covered,
Each molecule of sky.

An antidote they'd fashioned
To be fired into the clouds,
Every Pudding could all watch it,
It would be harmless to the crowds.

The scientist then fired upwards
And the darkness did disperse,
They no longer lived in blackness,
Freed from the evil of Lards curse.

The scientists they were honoured,
Each given the freedom of the town,
Presented with a trophy,
And a gold Black Pudding gown.

The Black Puddings worked together,
The last few days they tried to blot.
But the lessons learnt in darkness,
Were ones no one forgot.

PART TWO

Tommy the Tailor

Tommy the Tailor, such a well-meaning man,
Worked hard in his shop every day.
His motto "I must do the best that I can
To please more and more people each day".

Tommy the Tailor had worked many years,
Just doing the best that he could.
He'd work many hours, through good times and tears,
To make clothes that were better than good.

Tommy the Tailor's bell rang many times,
As customers came in through the door.
To choose colours, a mixture of blacks, whites and limes,
If they wanted, he'd always find more.

Tommy the Tailor met so many friends,
The number grew more every day.
He helped them with fashion, explaining the trends,
Finding time and a good word to say.

Tommy the Tailor's heart leapt in his chest,
When a lady walked into his store.
She had class, for she knew which style was the best.
He knew, of her, he would like to see more.

Tommy the Tailor grew to like her so much,
And he knew she was more than a friend.
Each time when he saw her, he wanted to touch,
But he was careful so not to offend.

Tommy the Tailor asked "Come for a drive?
We'll go for a ride in my car.
Let's go to the Lakes, we'll be home before five.
Or, maybe we won't go that far".

Tommy the Tailor was upset she laughed,
As she brushed his suggestion aside.
Was it a joke, or was it a part of his craft?
Did she know of his feelings inside?

Tommy the Tailor tried over again,
And hoped that she would change her mind.
He knew that on purpose she would not cause pain.
His attraction could not be denied.

Tommy the Tailor has listened one day,
as a personage known as St. Jude
was explained as a help in work, rest or play
helping those who are hungry find food.

Tommy the Tailor thought he'd have a try
And asked Jude if he would lend a hand.
Not wanting the chance to hold her, pass by.
But, if it did, he'd quite understand.

Tommy the Tailor stands all fingers crossed,
As he waits in a state of duress
He hopes that this chance will never be lost,
And her answer will finally be yes....

Tommy's Dream

The sun was shining as I wandered,
Birds were singing in the air.
When I walked down by the river
I looked up and saw them there.
They were standing in the meadow,
Multi-coloured, growing free.
There was one right in the middle
And I knew it was for me.

I just stood and kept on looking
At the beauty of the bloom.
There is not one eye existing
Which would refuse to give it room,
Then I saw her in the distance,
Sunlight glinting in her hair.
Complimenting all around her,
Causing me to stand and stare.

I watched her tripping lightly.
I watched her as she went by.
Butterflies which once were dormant
Choreographed across the sky.
All as one they danced together,
Gently floating to and fro
To the strains of silent music.
Such sweet melody, so slow.

I reached out and picked the flower
Which had stood out from the rest.
I knew that she above all others
Deserved nothing but the best.
So, I wandered over to her,
With the treasure in my hand,
Not wanting to offend her,
Hoping that she'd understand.

Dropping on one knee before her,
Holding high the bloom aloft,
It was then I saw how silky
Her skin was, and oh, how soft.
She said she had an answer
To a previous question asked.
It was one for which I'd waited.
I was to hear it now at last.

She held her hands out to me,
To lift me from the floor.
Then we walked in blissful silence,
Towards a vaguely distant door.
She turned her eyes upon me.
I tried to hear the words she spoke.
But it was at that very moment,
in great misfortune, I awoke.

I lay there with her vision.
The answer I could only guess.
But, the way her lips were forming,
it could only have been a yes.......
Now I live in trepidation,
Fighting away life's deep despair,
Spending all my waking hours,
As I search the land for her.

The Lady Replies

To Tommy the Tailor, the lady replies
"Though flattered (of that there's no doubt)
I think that the stars are clouding your eyes.
They'll clear, if you just blink them out.

Though infatuation is terribly nice
It gives one a flip, don't you just see,
It's hard to imagine, it really seems odd
That the object of passion is ME!!

The Lakes, they do sound inviting.
Your charm, could on me work a treat.
But...true to form, as always, I'm standing.
Firmly each day on my feet.

I didn't set out to capture.
I must have some well-hidden charm.
But, families they must be considered
And protected from possible harm.

The prospect it does seem exciting.
I tell you I never have dallied.
The truth of the matter is simply
I'm really, very happily married.

The poem is finally over.
As all good things must come to an end.
But Tommy, there is no reason
Why we can't we just remain friends."

Tommy Explains

I've considered your answer, and I do understand.
But I feel you should let me explain.
There was not one intention in my little plan
To make any one person feel pain.

I have known for a long time, I've been left in no doubt,
Of the importance of your family life.
It's abundantly clear and apparent to me
He's got a wonderful, first class ace wife.

But, when we met, you were different to me.
It's all true, there's no word of a lie.
You stood out from the rest that I served in my shop.
I used to watch you as you slowly walked by.

Each day that the cock crowed, I hoped you'd come in
And spend time, spending time just with me.
But I knew it was wrong for me even to hope,
All the time knowing you were not free.

It did not stop me longing. or wanting you near,
Knowing there was no chance you'd be mine.
But, I could not keep the state of my feelings inside.
I had to lay them all out on the line.

It would be nice in our case if we, as good friends,
Could go out for a ride or a meal.
Remembering restrictions, we have in our lives,
And controlling just how we might feel.

Infatuation is how you describe
The feelings I have towards you.
You're my central passion don't you understand.
Come stand where I am. see the view....

We can't understand, we can never explain
Just what happens to us every day.
The mysteries of life sometimes catch us off-guard,
Affecting us as we work, rest or play.

I have served many people, I have spoken to all
Who have stopped to spend time in my shop.
But until you came in, I'd never met one
Who I wished, for a long time she would stop.

I have flirted and laughed, serving folks, as I do,
To bring colour to lives painted grey.
But the words that I spoke meant nothing to me
Until I heard the bell ringing that day.

I wanted to tell you, oh so many things.
But I took time because walls do have ears.
So I bided my time till the right moment came
With restrictions as one of my fears.

There is one thing in life I cannot understand
But it's a rule that we all must obey.
When a boy meets a girl, they must both be aware
Of what people around them may say.

I have written a lot. I hope you're not bored.
So, I'll now bring this poem to an end.
There are very few people who'll ever become
As dear to me as you are, my friend.

If we never do take a ride out in the car,
Or just walk by the lake hand in hand,
I'll just count it as one of my losses in life,
But my lady, I do understand................

Tommy talks to the Black Pudding Soldier

Tommy the Tailor was looking so sad
as the Black Pudding Soldiers walked by.
"What's the matter with you, young Tommy me lad?"
Was the Sergeant Black Pudding's rough cry.

"That needle you lost in the old farmer's stack,
We'll find it I'm sure, come what may.
You'll soon have your needle to darn, sew and tack.
Let's go find it, come, what do you say?"

But Tommy just glanced up, and then shook his head,
At the Sergeant who was standing there close.
"Thanks for your concern" our sad Tommy said,
"But that's not the reason I'm feeling morose.

You see, I've met a young lady who captured my heart
The very first day that we met.
The heat in my body, to rise it did start.
If I was jelly I never would set.

But my love I don't think she'll ever return
For her feelings belong to another.
To look and not touch I'll just have to learn
And to be to her no more than a brother.

I've already asked her if there was a chance
That we could go out for a meal.
And, not being one to skirt round and dance,
I've told her how deeply I feel."

He told how she'd asked if they could be friends
With limits how close they became.
A long, long friendship which he hopes never ends.
Two actors in life's romance game.

"But I know that given a choice of a little or none,
The choice for me has surely been made.
I'd rather not find that all contact has gone,
But our closeness is merely delayed.

So, I'll continue to serve every day in my shop,
And look forward to when she comes in.
Then innocent words to her I will say
Awaiting time when the real words begin."

The sergeant just laughed. He'd helped Tommy find
A reason to continue with life.
This lady he'd met will still fill his mind.
A dear friend, but never his wife.

Tommy went back to his rightful place
In his shop, where each day he would stand.
Looking forward to when he would look at her face,
And dream of walking with her, hand in hand.....

Tommy the Philosopher

Every day I stand there in my shop
My customers they come in.
They pass the time and buy my wares.
A suit, a coat, a pin.

Each one has needs unique to them,
Each one has personal dreams.
They wear a mask for public chores.
A "life's not what it seems".

Each one has, desires so deep,
For wealth to change their lives.
For treasures that are out of reach
But, desire, ambition drives.

I see poor men in worn out clothes.
Their weathered and sallowed skin.
Uneasiness is in their eyes.
Clear to me as they walk in.

They look at the clothes that they'd like to wear.
The price for them is too high.
They put the coat carelessly back on the rack,
Then pass on slowly by.

They wish they had enough to spend
And throw their rags away.
Oh, will their fortune ever change?
They hope it will, someday

The rich, who have no need to want,
And wardrobes full of clothes,
Get tired of all the things they own,
Say "Send me some of those".

They talk of money that they invest
To make their wealth increase.
They always want to have some more,
And never finding peace.

Through history, there have always been
Men who went in search of gold.
They travelled constantly, far and wide.
The young, also the old.

They felt great hunger many times.
Their bodies racked with great pain.
They suffered like the pirates in days gone by
Who sailed on the Spanish Main,

They murdered, they robbed and took by force
Things that would make them so rich.
Believing soon the day would come
When from their own ship they'd unhitch.

Men gamble all their wealth away
Believing they will win
Enough to set them up for life
And good times will begin.

But each chase is impossible,
The goal posts they are moved.
Belief that wealth is all you need
Is many times disproved.

I hear of people making time,
To chase their "Pot of Gold".
Trying to find the precious jewels
To keep them from the cold.

But as I stand, I wonder at
The folly of it all.
I find my wealth in other things,
No fear when markets fall.

I've no desire for "Pots of Gold",
No fancy clothes to wear.
The thing I really treasure most
Is time I spend with her........

Tommy's Despondency

Tommy the Tailor, heart broken in two,
Has now lost the love of his life.
The person he'd choose to be one day his Queen.
The person he'd choose for his wife.

He'd seen her each day as she came through the door,
All her items of shopping to buy.
He'd fallen in love with her so pretty face.
He fell for the smile in her eye.

He'd taken her out after so many tries.
They'd gone for a walk by the lake.
He felt that he'd then found his partner for life.
But, today she has made a mistake.

He's shown all his love in the things that he did.
He told her with words he did say.
He felt such a closeness would never dispense,
And they'd live with each other one day.

But now, over weekend, fates taken a hand
And the pressures from family did rain,
They pressed for a chance to be given to him.
So she's given in to them, again.

She's gambled on trust that he'll change his life-style,
And her love - she's not sure if it's there.
She's gambled he'll keep to the things that he said
And he'll keep promises he made to her.

But Tommy the Tailor, apart at the time
When that fateful decision was made,
Has now to rebuild after being destroyed.
Rubble now, where foundations were laid.

Her decision is made, and it's one he'll respect.
But his love for her will never die.
So, he'll leave her with sorrow so full in his heart
And he'll leave her with tears in his eye.

His lonely life's trek he'll start without her.
For her face he will no longer see.
But he'll love her with every breath that he takes
And he'll dream of what might, and should, be.

The End, or the Beginning?

Tommy the tailor, alone in his store
Sat wiping the tears from his eye.
Would he ever again see his ladies sweet face,
Or smell her perfume as she passed so close by?

He just pondered on what was left for him,
Should he sell up and go far away?
Or should he put it all behind him,
Trying to forget that once fateful day?

The day when his life had new meaning,
The day when happiness began,
When he saw beauty in creation,
And he became an appreciative man.

He then appreciated beauty
And such sweetness so serene,
When he saw her walking past him,
She was the best he'd ever seen.

Just then a beam of sunlight flickered,
As the clouds began to break.
Why had the sun now started shining,
With his heart so full of ache?

Then the stores' door started moving
Its' creaking pierced the cold dark air.
As it swung wider & wider open,
He looked & saw her standing there.

In her hand she held a suitcase,
Some other bags down by her feet.
Were his eyes now being cruel,
On his emotions did they cheat?

He rubbed his eyes, he looked more closely,
It was her he felt so sure,
He rose with his arms wide open,
And ran to greet her 'cross the floor.

She'd like to share his life she told him,
If he still wanted her to stay.
He just held her tight and whispered,
"Don't you ever go away".

In the sky the sun shone brightly,
Its' rays covered all around,
The birds suddenly started singing,
Flowers spread covering all the ground.

In Black Pudding land there was a party,
People danced and people sang.
The church bells with glad tidings,
Rang out over all the land.

Now our Tommy has his lady.
She is the answer to his prayer.
And he knows he'll always love her,
If she's in trouble, he will be there.

We've reached the ending of our story,
But for them it's just the start.
They are rich beyond all measure,
They have love inside their heart.

PART THREE

Wilber.

Wilber cleaned the windows
In the streets throughout the town.
Each day holding his bucket,
He climbed up and he climbed down.
No matter what the weather,
You would see him working hard,
When the wind tried to dislodge him,
He would give it scant regard.

But one day, something happened,
As he placed his ladder on the ground,
He heard somebody shrieking,
It was a loud and piercing sound.
Looking around, he could see no one,
Although he turned both left and right,
Then he looked up and was so startled,
As he saw a disturbing sight.

Mrs. Jones from around the corner,
Was floating high up in the air,
Her hands clinging to her washing,
As birds nestled inside her hair.
He called, "What are you doing,
You shouldn't be so high,
If you don't come down this minute,
You'll go higher than the sky".

"How ever did you get there?
Now what are we going to do?
I must find the answer,
Of how I can rescue you".
She called out that she was hanging,
Her sheets onto the line,
When a gust of wind came blowing,
Even though the sun did shine.

Her sheets, seemed to be dancing,
As they flew unto the air,
With her holding on to the corners,
It did give her such a scare.
And now all she does is hover,
Floating on a gentle breeze,
Tears are seeping from her eyes and,
She really, really wants to sneeze.

"Hang on", said Wilbur bravely,
"There must be something we can do",
Then he took evasive action,
As Mrs. Jones lost her left shoe.
Just then around the corner,
The town fire engine did appear,
Driven by young Fred the fireman,
Who looked up and said, "That's queer".

"Whatever is she doing?
That's not the way to dry
Her washing, she must come down",
Then they heard a mournful cry.
"Please help me, I am tired,
And my arms they really ache,
I promise if you save me,
I'll bake a great big chocolate cake".

Fred and Wilbur stood there thinking,
About how best to proceed,
Then Wilbur said, "I've got the answer,
It is a great idea indeed.
Fred I'll climb onto your engine,
You hoist the ladder from the rack,
I'll climb up and try reach her,
With any luck, we'll bring her back".

Holding tight onto the ladder,
Making sure he was well secured.
Wilbur gingerly climbed upward,
Already tasting his reward.
At the top, he stretched his arms out,
As Mrs. Jones went drifting past,
He missed once, then twice then three times,
Then got hold of her leg at last.

Swaying with the wind he struggled,
But his grip was very strong,
He said, “Don’t worry missus,
I’ll have you down before too long”.
Keeping hold, he clambered downward,
Until they both were on the floor.
Mrs. Jones said, “I’m glad that’s over,
I couldn’t have held on much more”.

The three of them looked upward,
Watched the sheet floating away,
Wondering if their families would believe them
When they told the happenings of that day?
“You must both come around tomorrow,
And then I’ll give you your reward,
A freshly baked cream gateau
With the chocolate freshly poured”.

Big grins came on the faces
And their eyes were shining bright.
They knew what they would dream of
When they went to bed that night.
Suddenly the wind stopped blowing,
And the sheet began to fall,
Mrs. Jones then burst out laughing,
And then she wore it like a shawl.

JIMMY THE JANITOR

Jimmy the janitor walked down the street,
New hat on his head, new shoes on his feet.
No care on his mind, no worries had he
What a blessing the future he could not see.

Jimmy the janitor had a good life,
Three lovely children, a faithful young wife.
A house a garden an old Oak tree.
A nice rosy future have I thought he.

He did not know what lay ahead,
His plans had been made right.
Spent so much time to work them out,
They were all so water tight.
He'd a career
No need to fear.

Jimmy the janitor enjoyed such good health.
His own bank balance, but not too much wealth.
Had the same car for many a year
"I'm secure" said he, "I've no need to fear".

Jimmy the janitor's life was to change.
His comfort and plans would soon rearrange.
A young little girl with sin in her heart,
Decided the downfall of Jimmy she'd start.

She told how she was persuaded
To climb into his car.
When his hand did stray, she ran away
Before he went too far.
She even cried,
Although she lied.

Jimmy the janitor sat in the chair,
His fingers he constantly ran through his hair.
He sat in an office he'd just painted cream.
"This cannot be real, it must be a dream".

Jimmy the janitor heard what she'd said,
"It's not true, it's all lies", he said shaking his head.
Handcuffed and led by a man dressed in blue,
"We have places reserved for perverts like you".

What could he say? They all believed
He did those nasty things.
And his poor wife, how would she feel
When the household telephone rings
And hear him say,
He's locked away?

Jimmy the janitor sat on the floor.
His eyes blank, he stared at his locked cell door.
Thinking about all the things he had lost,
A young girl told lies, now he'll pay the cost.

Jimmy the janitor knew he couldn't face,
The ridicule, the shame and the deep disgrace.
The whispering voices, the sniggering sneers
The distrust of his neighbours, their lingering fears.

What could he say? Who would believe
The things she said were all wrong?
His poor wife, would she believe
He'd loved her all along?
She'd surely know.
He'd loved her so.

Jimmy the janitor, sat all alone
Doubts in his innocence hourly had grown.
All his so-called friends, as one turned their back.
No-one will defend him, they only attack.

Jimmy the janitor ripped off his shirt,
Put a noose 'round his neck, he pulled 'till it hurt.
With it tied to a bar, took his feet off the floor,
Jimmy the janitor, alas was no more.

The little girl who told the lie,
Knew, just what she had done.
It was just a joke, but it backfired.
She only wanted fun,
But she can't laugh,
No she can't laugh.
She just can't laugh

Helena Ready

Helena Ready, was marrying Freddie,
The morning after the ball.
A lavish affair, many were to be there
A response to the clarion call.

Directions were sought, the presents were bought,
Each believing their gift was the best.
The guests all set out, each one with no doubt,
They were better than all of the rest.

The wedding went fine and the sun it did shine.
Through the clouds as they all made their way
Very soon it went dark, as they entered the park
Where the reception was set out that day.

They all wrapped up warm, for it looked like a storm,
Was going to come down real soon,
Running into the tent, the one her father did rent,
They sheltered from the threatened monsoon.

Well it started to rain, and to nobody's gain,
The wind started blowing due East.
It blew quite a storm, turned cold soon from warm
And played havoc with all of the feast.

The cream from the gateaux spread high, then spread low.
It covered the candles and cake.
The bride and her mother, ran 'round like no other
How much more of it could they both take?

Then with one sudden blow it made more of a show
When it inflated the brides white lace dress.
High into the air & with rain wetting her hair.
She did look a terrible mess.

Up, up she did go as the wind it did blow
And she tangled with cables and trees.
While the birds in the air could do nothing but stare
At the poor girl who had started to freeze.

Up-up she went higher, above the church spire,
Where not too long before she was wed.
Her life quickly went past from first moment to last,
As memories were flooding her head.

With ice on her nose, no shoes on her toes
She wondered when her nightmare would end.
As she passed the bandstand, she reached out with her hand
Grabbed the flagpole & her weight made it bend.

As the wind blew all 'round it bent nearer the ground
She held on tightly with all of her might.
The wind stopped as she'd yearned, the pole upright returned
And she was catapulted into the night.

Like a bullet she flew and the hall came into view
As she started her speedy decline.
They 'd given her all up for dead, now with dress over her head
She'd returned like a heavenly sign.

As she flew through the air, people ran here and there
Not knowing which direction to take.
Then they all turned around as a soft squelchy sound
Told them she'd landed head first in the cake.

Her groom lifted her down rearranging her gown
As the people all started to cheer.
After embracing her mother, her bridegroom and brother,
She sat down as she came over all queer.

The party went on as her fear soon was gone,
She tried her best although still soaking wet.
This day no matter what reason, be it wedding or season
Was a day she would never forget.

MELVIN

Melvin the milkman was up before dawn
To load all his milk on the van
He made a great effort through good health and bad,
A hard-working dependable man.

I remember the time when the rain, pouring down,
Left puddles so deep in the road
And gave Melvin the milkman a difficult time
To keep safe his precarious load.

He started so slowly; you'd think he was stopped
But he gradually moved on through the rain.
He had to deliver the milk to his friends
For he looked forward to seeing them again.

Melvin drove on past the school and the church,
While the waters rose up to his seat.
He was trying so hard to see which way to go,
Unaware of his wet freezing feet.

In his electric blue van, he went safely through town,
And the water rose up to his chin.
Then he said to himself, "I'd better go back,
And my journey again I'll begin".

He carefully reversed to the place he'd begun
To dry off, and change all of his clothes.
He looked at his bottles, and shook sadly his head.
There seemed no answer to all of his woes.

With a warm cup of coffee gripped tightly in hand,
He thought sadly, "Oh what can I do?
My friends are all waiting, relying on me.
There must be some way to get through".

Then he stood in his workshop, and looked quickly around
Disliking the fact, he was late.
Then he spied in the corner four flat inner tubes,
"They'd be useful, if they would inflate".

Next, he spotted a pump, lying there on the floor,
And the hard work with vigour began.
"I've got to succeed in blowing these up.
Though it's tough, I'll do the best that I can".

He hurt as the blisters formed onto his hands
But he knew he could never give in.
"If I carry on pumping, the job soon will be done
And my deliveries again I'll begin".

As he continued to work, the rain kept falling down.
The flood waters unceasing did rise.
As he looked through the window, he said to himself,
"It'll soon reach right up to the skies".

At last he had finished. He sat back and smiled.
The time it was so close at hand.
When he'd leave his small dairy and deliver his milk,
He was late, but they'd all understand.

He jacked up the van, placed each wheel in a tube,
It looked like it was floating on air.
"In all of my years, I've not let them down.
They knew I would always be there".

Then he pulled on the rope that he'd tied to the door.
Through the opening the waters did flow.
As the level rose up, the van started to move.
Down the road towards town it did go.

How the people all cheered when they noticed our friend,
Floating down with his milk to deliver.
They were all so relieved that they quickly forgot,
How the rain made the cough, sneeze and shiver.

When his work was complete, Melvin started back home,
Relieved that his work was now done.
As he paddled on homeward, the rain clouds gave way
And he soon felt the warmth of the sun.

"At last", Melvin thought, as the storm came to an end,
And the waters flowed into the drain.
"It's been one of those days, when each thing goes wrong,
And you hope it won't happen again".

As Melvin sat down by the fire getting warm,
And the heat dried his shoes and his coat.
He laughed as he thought that for once in his life,
He had driven an actual milk "Float".

He continued to work, selling milk to his friends.
Everyday he was there on the dot.
And each time it rained, his mind still went back,
To the one day, that he never forgot.

Ballad of Brian and Ophelia.

What a peaceful Thursday morning,
My mind is all at ease,
I love it when I'm gnawing
A piece of my favourite cheese.

I've been sitting here for hours
Under skies turning to grey.
But there's nothing to disturb me
I can eat this cheese all day.

I found it on a large tin, flattened
By a humans heavy foot,
I must be careful of the edges,
Or my paws I'm sure I'll cut.

Deep in joy I didn't notice
That the dark has spread some more,
The shadows that were hovering
I couldn't see them anymore.

I look at trees now swaying
As a wind begins to blow,
I'm glad I'm a bit protected
Or else my cheese would surely go.

Ow! That rain drop seemed so heavy
When it landed on my head,
I should find myself some shelter
But I'll stay with my cheese instead.

Ow! More rain has started falling
Making puddles all around,
I'm amazed how very quickly
It has spread over the ground.

Oh, my cheese I must protect you
I will shelter you from rain,
For when it's stopped its falling,
I'll start to nibble you again.

Climbing on the tin I balance
Holding tightly with all claws,
I see some rubbish floating by me,
Gathering by some wooden doors.

Hold on what's that I am feeling,
It's a new experience for me,
I feel like I'm being lifted,
From the ground I no longer see.

There is water all around me,
The wind is blowing very hard,
I'm nearly knocked asunder
By a passing birthday card.

Round and round the current takes me,
I'm floating swiftly down the street,
I'm surely heading for disaster,
When Brian (the neighbour's cat) I meet.

"Hello Ophelia my dear how are you?
I've been waiting here for you.
I've made a reservation
And it's strictly for us two".

He salivates and dribbles,
From his perch high on a wall,
He stretches out to reach me,
But he slips and starts to fall.

Down he comes and lands right by me,
Water splashing in the air,
I hold on tight to ride the deluge,
I was so happy, life's just not fair.

The wind is getting so much stronger,
And the waters getting high,
I know the cats not happy
It's used to always keeping dry.

But he's still looking at his dinner,
Perched upon a piece of cheese,
Which is slowly getting thinner
Due to the pressing of my knees.

He reaches out to try and get me,
But he misses, claws the air.
Then tries to gain his balance
On the ground that once was there.

I watch the fear so slowly spreading
On once a fierce scowling face,
As the water drives us forward
Lifting us sometimes up in space.

Where will we stop? I have no notion,
Both cat and mouse are swirling free
We tumble through the darkness
When a splash of light I see.

The storm now's getting stronger
I'm sure we'll both be drowned,
There must be a chance of rescue,
So, I start to look around.

That splash of light is from an opening
Of a door standing ajar,
I wonder if I could reach it
It doesn't seem that far.

By myself I know I'll struggle,
I'll need the help of my new friend,
Who’s panicking near beside me,
I've no idea how this will end.

So, I point toward the opening
Indicating to go there,
When a wave hits and sends us crashing
High into the sodden air.

I land on something squishy
I slowly get up on my knees
When I suddenly feel disaster
I realise I've lost my cheese.

But my sorrow it is fleeting,
The light's still shining through the crack
When I'm suddenly aware
I'm riding on my new friends' back.

I gently tug upon his left ear
And direct him which way to go.
It takes ages to reach shelter
Fighting against the waters flow.

When we reach our destination,
And we tumble through the door,
I watch in quiet amazement
As my cheese falls on the floor.

e had saved my one possession,
The thing I held most dear,
He had grabbed it from the water,
As it floated very near.

Both exhausted wet and winded
Glad to now be safe and sound,
We made it with each other,
As locked in terror we were bound.

I saved him, and he saved me,
We'd both battled through the seas,
And the best part of the journey
Was my friend had saved my cheese.

We both slowly regained feeling
Sitting in puddles on the floor,
Knowing normal service will resume soon
And he'll be chasing me once more.

PART FOUR

The Builder

A leaf it fluttered to the floor,
Snapping off a branch up high.
The small boy watched in wonder
As a bird flew in the sky.
He saw it swoop and lift the leaf
Taking it to a nearby tree.
The boy he had to strain his neck,
To enable him to see.
The bird then stopped beside it's nest,
A new home for his kith and kin.
He watched it find a place to put the leaf,
And gently push it in.

ANTS

The window sill was covered by the ants,
They had marched down the road in droves,
A little boy bent down to play with the mites,
They ate him up, his skin and clothes all gone.
His bones were left, a glistening memory
Of the shape & form, the little lad used to be.
The gardens were left a desolate waste,
The bushes and geraniums all disappeared.
The wilderness behind, reminiscent of
An H-bomb blast remains.
And still they continued on.

An old woman shrieked and opened the glass,
To shoo the ants on their destructive way.
But they shuttled forward, and she fell over a chair.
Then the signal to advance was made.
Soon her carcase was pulsating black,
They were marching in and out of her eyes.
Her teeth or what were left all soon fell out,
As the flesh in her mouth was devoured.
After they'd finished, they left her bones,
They had sent her to meet her maker,
And still they continued on.

They marched through the house to a room up the stairs,
Where a young child so innocently slept.
Their blood lust was wetted by the victories just gained,
Now nothing can stand in their way.
To the door of the room they noiselessly crept,
Easily squeezing through the gaps in the wood.
They covered the cot & the child as it lay,
Then left it, unable to cry any more.
Just a sight to haunt its' mother for years,
And its' father to mourn for his child and its' mother.
And still they continued on.

The skull of a cat and its' skeleton bare,
Joined the list of the victims laid waste in their wake.
They devoured all things that dared stand in their way,
There was nothing that escaped the black savage hoard.
The army and policemen stood firm eyes aghast
As they observed the size of the enemy throng.
An armoured car was hidden from the view of all,
As the ants took control of events with such ease.
When they left, three young lads, not yet nineteen,
Were a mixture of bones, to be sent to their homes.
And still they continued on.

Scientists were working late into the night,
To find a way of destroying the scourge in the streets,
Flame guns they had used had limited success,
More men had been lost, martyrs, killed at their post,
Eaten alive while combating their foe,
The captains watched, as their men, trained to withstand nuclear attack,
Disappeared in front of them limb from khaki limb,
As the ants went in through their feet and out of their mouths.
Tasting victory with each morsel of flesh,
Devouring the blood not a fragment was left.
And still they continued on.

When daylight appeared and night bowed its' head,
The ants searched for shelter deep down in the ground.
It was time to relax after the previous hours,
When all effort was spent, out searching for blood,
It was the only thing that would appease their craving,
Cravings that started when chemicals escaped
From a wastage pipe of a factory nearby.
It seeped out to the fields where the ant kingdoms dwelt,
And caused the blood lusting to inspire their march.
Although fighting against this unnatural trait, they failed,
And still they continued on.

"Success cried the scientist when a formula was found,
And his many hard hours of toil brought reward.
The potion was sent to the air force nearby,
Which had planes standing ready to discharge the spray
On the ants to combat their longing for blood.
A report came in the ants had struck once again,
In a ward where bedridden patients did lie,
Unable to escape the onslaught of their doom,
As the ants made their way through, methodically cruel,
Nurses could only watch at the nightmarish sight.
And still they continued on.

Leaving the bones 'neath the sheets on the beds,
And fragments of bodies scattered over the hospital floor.
The ants made their way to a playground nearby,
Where children played, unaffected by the news.
Suddenly a noise in the sky, they watched the planes
rushing through,
To spray the potion that would save all mankind.
Down came the spray enveloping the black hoard.
And obscured it from the many anxious watching eyes,
For what seemed like an eternity, time slowly went by,
Until the mist faded, then revealed that no single ant,
Was alive to continue on.

ASHTON HOUSE

The silver spoons of Ashton House,
Made a jingling sound when disturbed.
It was like the sound of a china clock,
But the butler moved on unperturbed.
His job was to keep the spoons,
Always shining like the stars,
And the flowers would have a good nights' sleep,
For the spoons surround their vase.

The cobwebs gathered from room to room,
Dust had settled on the floor.
The maids now work in other homes,
And the house gets cleaned no more.
The butler he still stays loyal,
Though his masters' gone away.
They buried him just four months ago,
Now he's immersed in dirt and clay.

His last words to his butler,
Were "Come closer to me Jim,
Those spoons, you keep on cleaning,
Let them shine like a bright new pin".
So, the butler just keeps on cleaning,
Throughout the day and night.
But it is hard to keep them sparkling,
When lacking in your sight.

His skin is pale and very wrinkled,
And now he is getting very thin,
His insides' have all rotted,
Through drinking too much gin.
He's nearly dead, but he will not give up,
His work goes on and on.
Now I wonder who will find him,
For I'm sad to say, he's gone.

I guess there in his final resting place,
His work he will do faster,
For now, that he has gone there,
He will find his wealthy master.
The dust has gathered in Ashton House,
The spoons have all gone dim,
For they lack the ever-loving touch,
Of that faithful butler Jim.

The Cowboy Dilemma

How I love to watch the cowboys
In the films, out on the range,
They lived a life so perfect,
There is nothing I would change.
As I lie here in my garden,
Listening to the babbling stream.
I just allow my thoughts to wander,
And of my ideal life I'll dream.

Yes, I'd love to be a cowboy
Long ago in days gone by.
I'd be a loner with no family,
Just on myself will I rely.
My clothes would be pure buckskin,
Boots finest leather that's e'r been seen.
I'd ride a pure white stallion,
Across the range all lush and green.

I'd be such a friendly cowboy,
Meeting different folk each day,
We'd stop and have some coffee,
And in the sunshine, we would lay.
I'd tell them all of my adventures
Fighting bandits big and mean.
Hoping no one would ever ask me
How my clothes had stayed so clean.

I'd be a rootin' tootin' cowboy,
My six-gun ready by my side,
Bullets sitting in their chamber,
In case a rattlesnake I'd spied
Slithering slyly through the dirt tracks,
Looking for its daily prey.
My bullet would ring out sharply,
And then blow its' head away.

I'd be adventurous as a cowboy
Riding through deserts sparse and dry,
I'd smile as I watch the vultures
Soaring high up in the sky.
Salivating and assuming,
I'll be ready for their table,
But all they'll taste is disappointment,
When they realise I'm fit and able.

I'd be a brave and fearless cowboy,
Pretend I was the man of steel,
I'd be courageous and just ignore them,
And soon one by one away they'd peel.
I'd stare deeply into shadows,
To see if waiting bandits lie
Prepared to pounce upon a traveller,
And rob him, as he passes by.

I'd be a wary, watchful cowboy,
Keeping constantly aware.
Not daring to be complacent,
There may be danger anywhere.
At night lying by my campfire,
I'd hear coyotes howling loud.
Silhouettes against the moonlight,
Bodies low and heads held proud.

I'd still need comforts as a cowboy,
A roaring fire burning so bright.
It would keep me warm and cosy,
And keep the beasts away at night.
Sleep will slowly take me prisoner,
Taking all my cares away.
So warm and peaceful in the firelight,
I would in slumber, drift away.

Stars become companions of this cowboy,
Watching me from who knows where?
And the moon hovers like a mother
Cradling me in her silver care.
Her light will shine on creepy crawlies,
As they forage in the night.
Gathering food to feed their family,
Which are safe, hidden out of sight.

They won't stop 'cos I'm cowboy,
They'd still crawl deep inside my boots
While others climb inside my pockets,
And strip the skin from my Cheroots.
I'd be oblivious in my blanket,
As warm air, filters through the trees,
Not thinking of creepy crawlies,
Not thinking of the fleas.

But, what if it rained upon this cowboy?
Would I wake up soaking wet?
As I rushed around for shelter,
Would the trees be a safe bet?
I'd soon be standing in a marshland,
Puddles would suddenly appear,
Lightening would flash across the heavens
Cause my horse to bolt away in fear.

He will return, back to this cowboy,
I've fed him, groomed him, calmed his fears.
But my doubts begin to gather
As from sight he disappears.
I shove my things inside my blanket,
Then bravely, slowly make a start,
To search for my friend "Faithful",
Or he was 'til we did part.

I'd be a wet and tired cowboy,
Staggering through the dark and rain.
The weight of what I carried,
Would make my body ache with pain.
I'd have pains in many muscles,
I did not even know I'd had,
I'd suffer such exhaustion,
My head would spin and feel so bad.

When daylight comes this tired cowboy,
Would take a look across the land.
And as I saw no life was stirring,
My bags would drop out of my hand.
So I'd sit down on a boulder,
With the rain still falling down,
Not knowing which way to venture,
Or how far was the nearest town.

It would be a dripping, sodden cowboy,
Watching the sun rise in the sky,
But I'd soon feel very sticky,
As my clothes begin to dry.
The sun would keep on getting hotter,
And start to burn down on my back,
And so I'd dive back into shelter
To hide from the sun's attack.

Soon I'd be a hungry cowboy,
So I'd reach for the bag of beans
Which I'd wrapped inside my blanket,
I'd have no time to cook my greens.
But as I held the bag before me,
I just could not believe my eyes.
They had received a real good soaking,
When the rain fell from the skies.

So this disillusioned cowboy,
Acknowledged the rain had done quite well,
Instead of a bag of solid beans,
There was now a gooey gel.
I'd throw the bag into the bushes,
I'd scream out loud and pull my hair.
I'd throw my coat I'd throw my saddles,
And fire my bullets into the air.

I start to question being a cowboy.
Their life was really not that good.
They'd have rain and wind and thunder,
As well as fleas' that drank their blood.
Their horses would run away and leave them,
Leave them stranded. Oh! What joy.
Now I've changed my mind completely,
You can keep being a cowboy

Political Choices

Each one must make a choice,
No-body can escape,
They are bludgeoned each day from side to side,
By intellectual rape.
The T.V. and the papers,
Are used in this vile task,
Bureaucratic gargoyles
Put on a friendly mask.

They are using all deception,
To make you think they are your friends,
But manipulations used,
Reveal they all have different trends.
You switch on the television,
They smile at you through their false teeth.
Telling you that you pay too much tax,
And promise you relief.

They paint a pretty picture,
Flowery scented prose,
"You will only waste your vote,
If you vote for one of those".
So, they lay their biased point of view
Out onto the kitchen floor.
"It is wrong to have rich people,
Subsidised by all the poor".

"Vote for us", they say, not feeling,
"We'll rearrange the plan.
Give more money to the poor,
We promise you all, we can".
The smile they have's soon fading,
When the broadcast does conclude.
You feel they should apologise,
Their intrusion, it was rude.

You've heard all that they've said before,
To you they're all the same.
They tend to think your freedom,
Is part of their little game.
They ply you with temptations,
Trying to ensnare your vote,
So you can put them into office,
Then they'll turn and grab you by the throat.

Each day the power you have to purchase,
Does gradually decrease,
You are buying less and less items,
Soon your shopping trips will cease.
What then should you be doing?
You are wavering to and fro.
The loaded dice is in your hand,
And it's a dice that you must throw.

The manipulators have done their job,
Your mind is now a complete mess,
Many attempts you make to say "No",
But it always comes out "Yes".
Filled with fear to change your mind,
You are afraid to make a choice.
You feel one day you should protest,
But you always lose your voice.

Entering the polling station,
For registration of your vote.
An X you put upon your form,
With a lump inside your throat.
Each way you turn, you feel you've lost,
But still you must decide,
No matter how you make your choice,
You'll be taken for a ride.

The Bomb

A group of people stood and stared
At the man from whom they'd heard,
Their world would end at ten to nine
And at half-past eight, there's not much time.
Each one stood still, with open mouth,
The bomb would come in from the south.
No-one spoke, none made a sound,
Each one was rooted to the ground.

Then a youngster stirred and gave a cry,
"Mummy, I don't want to die".
"But who does?" The stranger said,
"Each person here, will soon be dead".
Panic spread just like a fire,
People all struggling in the mire.
Children stood on or pushed away.
They're not wanted, not on this day.

People running, crying aloud,
Looking closely at each cloud.
Some they stop to loot around,
Still wanting riches, from the ground.
No principles in life have they,
Greed chases all their fear away.
Like Egyptians they just want to store,
All their goods, and look for more.

Believing one day they'll return
No-more for worldly goods to yearn.
They continue oblivious to the noise,
The screaming and crying of girls and boys.
The shouting of people the stamping of feet
Running from the doom they'll all soon meet.
People are trampled, pushed aside,
A smile on some faces, relieved they'd died.

It's quarter to nine, the noise it clears,
Time goes slow, five minutes, five years.
All at once, a sound is heard,
There in the distance, a small white bird.
Some people stand, some they kneel,
Telling God how sorry they feel
For living lives with tight closed eyes,
Cheating, stealing and all those lies.

Tears are streaming quickly down each face,
As they bow to God and ask his grace.
Suddenly the bomb descends,
To the town on its' way it wends.
People huddle, they say "Good-bye".
The thought of death makes many cry.
Some fall flat upon their belly,
Good bye John", "I love you Nellie".

Vibrations spread across the floor,
A sickening thud, a deafening roar.
All have been hit, all are gone.
"Darling, darling, wake up John,
You're dreaming again, you're full of sweat,
It must have been the worst one yet".
John looked at Nellie, and gave a smile,
And lay back thinking, for quite a while.

DEAD?

I wonder if they'll notice,
They're standing all around.
My wife, my child, my mother.
Making a weeping, mourning sound.

The stethoscope upon my chest,
Can't hear my beating heart.
If someone does not notice soon,
My funeral they will start.

Machines around are bleeping,
Lights flashing white and red.
The answers are all negative,
I hear doctors said, "He's dead".

I'm not! I hear you talking,
I can see what's going on.
My wife she's really crying,
She's turned, she's walking. Gone.

The room has all gone quiet,
I'm lying here quite still.
I never thought that this would happen,
Why did I take that pill?

The professor said be careful,
Then he moved the drugs around.
"Don't take 'till we investigate
And see what side effects are found".

The drug had been invented
To help with all the common good.
It was to wipe out all diseases,
Or at least they thought it would.

I just stood there thinking, looking.
And thought, "I can be the first".
So, I took it swallowing quickly,
Then I thought my brain had burst.

In my head loud cymbals crashing,
Loud trumpets, blaring in my ears.
Bright lights around me, colours flashing,
I'd seen nothing like it in all my years.

I fell down lungs breathing heavy,
My body twisted, wracked in pain.
I looked up at the bottle,
And said "Never again!"

I lay there for some moments,
There was nothing I could do.
The professor cried as he came in,
"Jim! What is up with you?"

He bent down and tried to lift me,
But I was dead weight in his hands.
My mind told my body to get up,
But it ignored all of my commands.

"Oh, come on Jim, what have you done?
I only wish I knew.
Then maybe I could get something
That will help to revive you".

He looked around in deep despair,
The clock had just struck one.
Then he saw the pills upon the bench,
And one of them had gone.

"You silly fool I told you,
I said leave them alone".
He 'phoned to fetch an ambulance,
And its' siren soon did drone.

It brought me here to have some tests,
The driver moved so fast.
I did not know then, but that quick ride,
Would almost be my last.

The doctors back, his face looks sad,
I wish I could shout out,
"I am not dead, I am alive,
Of that I have no doubt".

I'm moving towards the mortuary,
I'm placed upon a slab.
I've oft been here in days gone by,
To fetch specimens for the lab.

Now I am here, I'm very scared.
There is nothing I can do.
I know someone soon will wrap me up,
When their examinations through.

How I wish I could communicate,
My mind is still awake.
Examine me again please, please.
Examine for goodness sake.

The drug it killed my body,
No sensations can it feel.
Please tell me that I'm dreaming,
Please say it isn't real.

They are starting now to bind me up,
I feel them pulling tight.
If I was to have senses remaining,
Oh, why were they my hearing and my sight?

I wish I could give my sight up,
I'd rather have my voice.
I would shout aloud, "I am alive",
And my family would rejoice.

Instead they're sad, they think I'm dead,
Oh, what a bad mistake.
I'm sure they'd find out I am alive,
If some more tests they'd only make.

They've finished up the binding,
My head is just left free.
They've just wheeled in a coffin,
Oh no! Is that for me?

Don't pick me up, don’t put me in.
How I wish that I could move.
Just one flicker of my eyelid,
Would my existence prove.

They have picked me up, and put me in.
The lid is placed on top.
I heard them say they could take me home,
And there tonight I'll stop.

They have wheeled me out quite slowly,
And placed me in a hearse.
I hear my family give their sad thanks,
To the doctor and the nurse.

They thank them for all their efforts
"You really tried your best.
But still you could not stop him,
Going to his final rest".

What are the words they're saying?
I am not really dead.
If only they would take a look.
They would eat the words they've said.

It is dark inside this coffin.
No light in here at all.
I cannot see up to the top,
The bottom, or the wall.

The hearse is moving forward,
What am I going to do?
It won't be very long before
The church doors I'll go through.

It is getting very stuffy now,
The air is getting thin.
What relief I'd feel if I could make a hole
With just a little pin.

I wish that we would get home,
The ride is very, very long.
I can't believe what now has happened,
My life has all gone wrong.

We have stopped, the door has opened.
I feel the coffin slide,
It's being carried by the handles,
Now they are taking me inside.

I must be in the parlour,
I suppose it is here where I will stay.
This room is where the children,
Spend lots of time to sit and play.

The lid is off they are looking in.
Oh, why can they not see
This is not an empty corpse,
Yes really, it is me.

Please dry your eyes you mourners,
It is really out of place.
You don't mourn when someone's living,
Just look into my face.

If you look at me very closely,
Just look into my eyes.
You'll find out I am still living,
In a body full of sighs.

The lights are dim, it must be late
They're all in the next room.
I need to show some signs of life,
And it really must be soon.

What's that did I hear some laughing,
Don't tell me someone told a joke?
It sounded like my cousin Paul,
I hope that on his drink he'll choke.

Darkness is all that I can see
As I look straight ahead.
Oh, why isn't there some little way
I can show them I'm not dead?

Wait! What is that noise? There's banging,
Someone's banging the front door.
A voice I hear and recognise,
It's my boss Professor Moore.

The lights are on, my wife is up.
Professor Moore has just burst in
There's so much talk and gabble,
They are making so much din.

The lights' on in the parlour,
Now they are standing all around.
It's gone quiet, now no-ones talking,
Wait what is that chinking sound?

I see a hypodermic
It's stuck now in my vein.
I've got a weird sensation,
I can feel my arm again.

The sensation, it is spreading,
It flows 'round with all my blood.
I'm beginning to feel quite normal,
I feel now just like I should.

I can move my arm; I can move my leg.
I've just moved my head around.
My mouth I have just opened,
It's a strain to make a sound.

"I am not dead", I've shouted,
"Please someone lift me out,
Such a long time in this coffin,
I just want to walk about".

I kiss my wife, & hug my kids.
It's handshakes all around.
I even hug my mum in law,
Then pat and stroke my hound.

"Oh, Jim you're very lucky",
The professor shook my hand.
"It's the mice on the desk you have to thank,
Those tied with the plastic band.

I was sitting so despondent,
Thinking, pondering your plight.
Mixing up some new chemicals,
Just waiting out the night.

I then emptied the hypodermic,
Into a mouse, dead, or so I thought.
It was treated with the formulae,
The one which tragically you were caught.

As I emptied out the needle,
And the fluid flowed right in.
I just sat there watching,
Then the movement did begin

I sat up quick and quite startled,
We believed that they were dead,
I was prepared to burn the carcase,
But I let them loose instead.

I checked out just what had happened,
I then researched into the pill.
It attacks the nervous system,
And makes you lie quite still.

It forms a kind of protective shield,
All around your vital parts,
It takes away all movement,
And all signs of life departs.

That is why we could not tell,
While you were lying on the bed,
That you were still quite alive,
We believed that you were dead".

Through the night time hours we partied,
Food and drink are flowing free.
The tension soon it takes its' toll,
And its' bed time now for me.

I'm tired & drifting into sleep now,
Silence engulfs at last my house,
Who'd have thought I'd owe my life
To the movement of a mouse.

PART FIVE

Too Late

A mother's sitting weeping for her baby, man of arms,
Who had heard the call and went to fight the foe.
Her memories reliving all the happy times gone by,
The songs of laughing children, alas so long ago.
Her eyes are misty, gazing at the photographs spread
On the table with untouched breakfast and cold tea.
"I want my little baby to walk once more through the door
To smile, say hello, spread his arms and cuddle me".

Fearfully she listens to broadcasts on the hour
Heart increasing beating, struggling with her breath.
In fear and trepidation until the man behind the desk
Reports "Terrorist action cause carnage and more death",
She feels the palpitations the cold sweat upon her brow
As his words meander through the tumult in her mind
The dead and injured names are read with solemn voice.
Her hands are white with fingers tight entwined.

She has not heard his name could it be he was not there?
Had he left before the terrorist attack?
Remembering her sorrow when he finally packed his bags
Oh, how she wished her loving only son was back.
Each scripted cold announcement from the ministry of
defence,
Cuts a deepening laceration in her heart.
As she thinks of all the families who only have just heard,
Their child was dead and now their world has blown apart.

Grief grows like a mushroom encompassing their soul
Filling each and every crevasse with its pain.
The child they loved and cherished will never return
They'll never see their cheeky face again.
She stands nervously, shaking like a leaf upon a tree,
Her blood pressure rising upward through the roof.
She did not hear her sons name, he was not on the list,
But she cannot feel relieved and that's the truth.

She's happy and she's guilty, mixed emotions swirl inside,
Her son lives, but another mother's child is lost.
Leaders say the daily price is one they'll gladly pay,
But families are the ones who meet the cost.
How many more will suffer for a war that no one wants,
Although they say it's a war that we must win.
To be prepared for losses the price it may be high,
They're not there to comfort when the sufferings begin.

The cancer of the unknowing slowly eats away
At the hope we once embraced deep in our soul.
And only when her son returns back to his home,
Is when her fractured family will again be whole.
What's that pain that's slowly spreading in her chest,
Uncomfortable tingling travelling down her arm?
Her vision's getting hazy her speech is sounding slurred,
Preventing her from raising the alarm.

Lying on the floor she tries to raise her aching head,
She drifts alternatively through consciousness and pain,
She's all alone and crying with one thought in her mind,
Will she ever see her only son again?
She's started feeling cold now, it's getting very dark,
The damp is creeping through her body from the floor.
Is it her imagination, she hears a friendly voice?
The sound of heavy feet from her front door?

Suddenly, she feels embraced, tears slowly sliding down
her cheek,
Hears caring words so softly spoken in her ear.
Her son's happiness he had when he was granted leave,
Has changed now to an emotion of deep fear.
He's been counting all the days to when he would return,
Back to the homely place where his life did begin,
A place of memories of much happiness and joy,
But now there's only sadness he has found within.

She knows it's time to leave, although she wants to stay,
She's waited longingly each day to see his face.
But her heart is beating slower, it's now time for her to go,
Her time has come, she's left the human race.
A son is sitting weeping for his mother in his arms,
Many years away, many miles they've been apart,
Too late to reminisce over memories they've shared,
Memories he'll hold forever inside his heart.

We Will Remember

A swirling mist, A boggy ground,
Slow progress in the ranks.
The smell of Sulphur in the air,
Surrounds the battered tanks.

Some men they limp, they have one leg,
Limbs lost in days gone by,
They find it hard keeping up the pace,
They fail, although they try.

Their pain is bad, it cuts through deep.
No relief in sobs or sigh.
Some soldiers hide emotions deep,
Others openly, unashamedly, cry.

There are those whose arms are ripped and torn,
With bandages tied 'round tight.
But through loss of blood, and weakened flesh,
Some die throughout the night.

Their bodies left, men scared to stop
Afraid of being lost.
They intend to keep their place in line,
No matter what the cost.

Fear it fills each trembling soul,
Their heads are bowed down low.
Their hearts no longer filled with pride.
Despair is all they know.

Their minds run on, they think of home,
Accepting it is not near.
The warmth of welcome that awaits them all
Is imagined very clear.

War's despondency leaves a bitter taste,
Rolling loosely around the tongue,
It lies so heavily in the gut
And pollutes inside each lung.

The group of men, who struggle back,
Just some of those who went.
Are trudging slowly, full of woe.
Bones weary and backs bent.

Tears are seeping from tired eyes.
The shame of their retreat
Is added weight to weary legs,
And a hindrance to their feet.

Then suddenly, the air turns green,
It is swirling 'round their head.
The men up in the leading ranks,
Have collapsed, they've joined the dead.

The gas it spreads, affects each one,
No-one escapes its' touch.
Some men they try, to hold their breath,
But the effort is too much.

When the air it clears, no soldier stands,
Each one has met his end.
No-one is left to prepare the dead,
Or their funerals to attend.

Eventually, the news spreads home,
And is received with deep regret.
"Collateral damage", the generals say,
"Will not spoil the best war yet".

A mother sits and waits in fear,
For news of her brave son.
Who left his home when duty called,
And picked up his army gun.

She does not know, he's lying dead,
He never will return,
She'll never hold him in her arms,
Oh! How much her love does burn.

Around the country, tables set,
For a celebration meal.
But, no joy now lives in any heart,
Tribulation is all they feel.

Fathers, sons and brothers gone,
Uncles, and cousins too.
Sacrificed for a moral cause,
Giving their lives for me and you.

We always will remember them,
And all that they did give.
Because of those who gave their lives,
In freedom we can live.

How Ever

However, can we thank them,
Those who for freedom gave their all?
Leaving behind their home and comforts
When they heard the bugle call.

No thought for their tomorrow,
They just believed in their today.
"We'll be home before you know it",
They sang as they marched away.

But things were oh so different
When formed in their battle lines,
Instead of thoughts of valour,
Fear and trepidation filled their minds.

In fields of mud and debris,
Blood flowed amongst the flowers.
They all stood together fighting,
As the minutes turned into hours.

Around them comrades falling,
Mouths closed, screams they tried to smother,
But soon the pain took over,
As they called out for their mother.

Ranks continually ordered forward,
Preventing men to aid their friend,
They were living through a nightmare
In a war that seemingly won't end.

Men were killed or left disabled,
Paying the price to live in peace,
As their days turned into years,
They prayed for their war to cease.

When it did, they all marched homeward,
Those without legs on stretchers high,
Bittersweet the taste of winning,
Remembering friends now in the sky.

So many men were badly injured,
And so many useful lives were lost,
Minds now filled with disturbing nightmares,
Asking was it worth the cost?

In every home that filled with laughter,
There were many homes that mourn,
As in tears the families sorted
Unwanted clothes that had been worn.

We all now enjoy our freedom,
Due to the price then paid,
By those who fought their battles,
May their sacrifice, not be betrayed.

So, how ever will we thank them,
Who for us have given all,
And who sacrificed their futures,
When they heard the bugle call?

Let us remember all the fallen,
And all those who walked away,
But still are suffering in silence,
A dreadful price they had to pay.

When we stand with heads bowed, silent,
Let us give all the thanks we can,
Remembering all those heroes,
Be they woman, child or man.

We All Lose Somebody Sometime.

We all lose somebody sometime,
When their life's journey is at an end.
Then we'll remember all the memories,
The good times spent with a friend.

We all lose somebody sometime,
It's when they finally close their eyes,
And their spirit leaves their body,
Floating up beyond the skies.

We all lose somebody sometime,
A family member or a friend.
And though they live as it won't happen,
The life they live one day, will end.

We all lose somebody sometime,
When we'll no longer hold their hand,
Whispering words of sweet affection,
And words of love they understand.

We all lose somebody sometime,
So, value everyone you know,
Don't take anyone for granted,
Spend time with them before they go.

Don't regret the missing closeness,
Or precious moments so sublime,
Don't be left with lonely sadness,
We all lose somebody sometime,

PART SIX

THE JOURNEY

I walked down the road with my head held high,
I fell in a puddle and I gave a sigh,
And said "On this idea I am not too keen".

As I walked down the road I was looking low
And very soon I shouted loudly "Oh! No!"
A wall had been built where it shouldn't have been.

Well I looked around, & walked back and fro,
But my feet didn't know which way to go.
I was slipping on a pool of gasoline.

So I looked ahead & then looked up & down
To see if I was in a country or in a town.
I was surprised to be standing in between.

There were two of us when we started out?
I am now alone causing me to doubt
My close friend for a while I hadn't seen.

So I jumped up landing on the branch of a tree,
And I looked high & low while trying to see
If a bird would take an epistle to the Queen.

Then I flapped my arms & started to fly,
And soon I was much higher than the sky.
Where the air was nice and fresh and clean.

So I soared on & on twisting 'round & around
So fast I couldn't even see the ground.
When I stopped, on the sun I had to lean.

Then I fell to the earth with a heavy bump,
And I landed inside a camels hump.
Boy was he so angry and so very mean.

I waited 'till the pyramids came into view
Before deciding what next I was to do.
The view was so peaceful & very serene.

But the camel kicked and I flew fast through the air
I got sand in my eyes in my toes & my hair.
Sand was in places where it shouldn't have been.

When I stopped, I stood up then gave a shake,
Felt my bones in pain, for I truly did ache.
The pain was so real, but the bruise unseen.

Then I went for a swim in a puddle nearby,
I'd thought I'd be wet, but the water was dry.
It was at the bottom of a very deep ravine.

Up I stood, nice & bright, then walked to the shore,
I looked for the puddle which alas was no more.
I found a mirror & my hair I did preen.

Then suddenly there right before my eyes,
A baker had started to bake some pies.
His outfit was blue with a lining of green.

Well he gathered up mice & he gathered up moss.
When he minced them up they looked like candy floss.
Then he added a cup of strong looking caffeine.

He offered me a piece, but I did decline,
It would go into a mouth, but it would not be mine.
The time had come for my trip to reconvene.

So I jumped on a horse that was trotting nearby.
And the man disappeared inside his own pie.
The crust it was burnt and the meat wasn't lean.

Then I gee'd up the horse & it started to run.
Heading back to the place from where I had begun.
But too late did I see my good friend Jean.

Well her bones they did crack as she fell to the ground,
From her mouth came a choked & a gurgling sound.
And her face looked just like gelatine.

As I looked down, I thought I shouldn't be here.
There was something not right, and to me it was clear.
I had a desire for a distinct change of scene.

With my feet I did kick, and the horse it did bolt
I held on for dear life and it gave me a jolt,
As its coat smelt just like nicotine.

Then he ran up a hill & had not gone far
When he started climbing up the beams of a star.
It's form was so heavenly and so serene.

The moon said "Hello" as she floated nearby.
Cocked her head, pursed her lips gave a wink of her eye.
She looked like a princess, no, more like a queen.

My eyes they were glued to her sweet shining face
As my horse continued its' ride up into space.
But I was drawn like a magnet & started to lean.

I leaned far too far and then started to fall
I slipped from my horse & in fear I did call.
But my horse carried on and soon was unseen.

I tumbled on down, very lost in the dark.
I fell past a swallow a duck & a lark
I must have been the strangest bird they had ever seen.

Well I bounced on the earth, and rebounded again,
I bounced into sunshine, and then bounced into rain.
I felt ill as my face turned evergreen.

Then I caught my right foot in a telegraph wire,
It restricted my rise, stopped me getting much higher.
There were two and my head got stuck in between.

I just dangled awhile being caught by my hair.
People gathered below & could just stand there & stare.
They asked what I was doing & what did I mean?

They called me to jump, but deep down I was scared.
I ignored & pretended I just hadn't heard.
Except for the voice of my sister Eugene.

She fetched a coloured balloon & she blew it up hard.
With a long piece of string it was tied to a card
She wrote on a few words, & one was obscene.

She said if I curled myself up into a ball.
I'd untangle my hair then to earth I would fall.
This was something else on which I was not too keen.

I just knew where I was, I did not want to stay.
I had hung by my hair for what seemed more than a day.
I wanted another distinct change of scene.

So I did what she'd said, & she was right, I did fall.
The crowd who had stared, gave a cheer one & all.
Except the man who looked like a Heinz baked bean.

I just stared as I fell and he gave me a smile.
One tooth in his head like a cracked bathroom tile
It was yellow & black not a little bit clean.

I looked at his hands, he was holding a bath,
This he swung to his left, then right into my path.
Across the top was a big magazine.

It was big, it was strong, and it did break my fall.
I was catapulted back up and straight into a wall
And slipped down head first into the mincing machine.

The short-sighted butcher mistook me for beef,
But his wife put him right much to my great relief,
But it was short lived as his eyes started to gleam.

"There's reluctance to beef since that thing C.J.D.
And an answer to prayer is just coming to me."
Then a snip of his idea she started to glean.

With my head still stuck fast, and my feet in the air,
They discussed his idea much to my great despair.
While I languished in meat and gelatine.

Then his hand moved quite fast to a switch on the wall.
Fear ran through my bones, and I started to bawl.
He said "We've started, we'll have to finish Christine".

Then a voice shouted "Stop!". I heard steps cross the floor
A police siren it wailed outside of the door.
A welcome sound although to me was unseen.

A hand pulled at my leg and I crashed to the ground.
I was shocked dazed and scared looking slowly around,
Then my eyes fell on a knife its condition pristine.

My hand slid along till the handle was tight,
And I decided to send them to their long dark night,
To reside with the bad men, evil and mean.

But the policeman said "No", and shook slowly his head,
"It profits you not if they both end up dead.
We have more ways than 'Madam Guillotine'.

So I walked slowly away to get on with my life,
Then I remembered my chid and my loving young wife.
Would she believe all the places I'd been?

I decided to tell not even one soul
A part of what happened never mind the whole.
They wouldn't believe what I'd done touched and seen.

And so safe and sound in my hospital bed,
I awake with the images still in my head.
I'd better go tell King Constantine.

So I skip into the garden, and talk to the flowers.
I sit there and tell them for hours and hours
Till the shadows across the grass do lean.

Soon the nurses they come and tuck me back into bed,
They give me some tablets, and stroke my tired head,
Then attach me to a bag of clear saline.

I soon fall asleep and once more start to dream,
Of new places and adventures as yet unforeseen
Dressed in my gown made of crisp polythene.

The Man

What's that noise? What can it be?
There's a man over there and he's looking at me.
He's stood in the dark in the shade of the trees,
With his long black coat hanging down to his knees.
He's smiling at me with a big toothy grin.
His hair is long and he's ever so thin
What does he want with me?

What's that noise? What can I see?
That man over there is coming to me.
He's holding a bag in his out-stretched hand,
He's mumbled some words I just can't understand.
His voice is quiet and his words aren't clear'
I'll just go stand closer so that I can hear.
What does he want with me?

I hear his voice; does he know me?
There's a pup in his car he has asked me see.
It's down on the floor curled up just like a ball,
It will lift up its head if I'd just only call.
But what's happening now? I just don't understand
His fingers are tight, and he's hurting my hand.
I cry but he does not hear.

It's gone so dark; I just cannot see.
There's a bag on my head and it's smothering me.
I let out a scream clearing the trees of the birds,
My ears they both ring and I can't hear his words.
Ouch! He's hit me now and I feel great pain
I'll feel some more if I scream loud again.
But I don't want to go with him.

I need some help! Is somebody there?
Will somebody help? Does that somebody care?
I hear somebody's voice it's loud and it's clear,
Now that somebody's running and he's coming quite near.
I hear the man swear, and then I'm pushed to the floor
I hear the man run and the slam of a door
I'm not going to go with him.

A hand lifts the bag! Pulls it high off my face.
Somebody's breathing quite hard like he's run in a race.
I look in his eyes see the swell of the tears,
I hear his warm voice trying to calm all my fears.
The bad man has gone, with this good man I'm free.
He smiles and he laughs, now he's cuddling me
I' m safe in the arms of my dad.

MIND

The weary body sinks in sleep,
Worn out by toil of day,
The cares and worries that were so real,
Have all thankfully flown away.

The mind is floating here and there,
Exploring through strange lands.
It joins in dances on the plains,
And plays in big brass bands.

It shows bravery where danger lurks,
Its' strength is second to none.
The memories all come floating back,
Of things here and things gone.

It finds its' self being chased by gangs,
Always stays one step ahead.
It feels the fear of being pursued,
Near caught, it is utter dread.

It looks for some way to escape
Eventually one is found.
Once through the door, the mind it finds,
Its' feet on friendly ground.

Soon more adventures come in view,
A jungle path to trek,
Or is it a case of swimming down,
To search a sunken wreck.

There are no bounds to keep it in,
On earth or out in space.
Its' strange we never see its' bulk,
Or look upon its' face.

It travels it seems for years and years,
With lots of tales to tell.
But it never beats that calling power,
Of that daily wakening bell.

LIFE FROM A PARK BENCH.

Sitting on a park bench
Watching the world as it goes by.
Observing people's nature,
Some are outward, some quite shy.
Some splash right through the puddles,
Some walk around the edge.
Some stepping on the pave stone,
Some tripping on the ledge.

Some sit there eating chocolate,
And some people have a smoke.
Some walking around quite quiet,
And some laugh, enjoy a joke.
Some old on sticks are leaning,
Trying to see, their necks, they crane.
Forever walking uphill,
Their leg muscles really strain.

Reflecting on their past life,
Despairing of the young.
Speaking of wars, they've fought in,
And of all the songs they've sung.
They say the youth think they're grown up,
Trying to be older than their years.
They show misguided courage
While they hide their buried fears.

They're impatient for tomorrow.
No time for yesterday.
Instead of ageing gradually,
As grown-ups some do play.
The rich they wear their new clothes,
Looking down upon the poor.
If some have to do a kindness,
They regard it as a chore.

A child with ice cream melting,
Stands crying on the path.
His clothes are torn and tattered,
He looks in need of a good bath.
His mother now has found him,
His eyes are nice and dry.
He's running, jumping, laughing.
Nothing now can make him cry.

As darkness falls the people,
Back to their empty homes they seep,
Be it a mansion or a hovel,
Inside their beds, they soon will sleep.
Their memories go with them,
Images forming in their head,
Travelling away on distant journeys,
Without leaving their bed.

The Mighty Pen

I made an old lady cry today,
I told her that her daughter was going away.
She was taking her family to another town,
She needs a place she could calm down.

I made an old lady smile today,
Her daughter said she was coming to stay,
She was bringing her dog and the children too,
She had things to tell her old and new.

I made an old lady laugh today,
I told her about a sunny day
When the grandkids played and ran around
Until they all fell rolling on the ground.

I made an old lady frown today,
Telling her in her house she could not stay.
Her payments were nowhere up to date
For her to make amends, it was just too late.

I made an old lady cry today,
I said a van would come take her away,
She would leave her home and memories there
And start her new life in social care.

In another life I began a war,
When people fought while tempers soar.
I told them they had to prepare
And when it all began; I was not there.

Over time I caused the war to end,
As surrender notes around they'd send.
The victors they had all the spoils,
The defeated bowed before the royals.

I broke a lovers' heart today,
Their love wanted them to go away.
I told them to leave and find another,
After going home to live with mother.

I filled a life with joy today,
I turned the skies to blue from grey.
A baby child had just been born,
A grandchild on this happy morn.

I've been around for many years,
I've spread some smiles and spread some tears.
I've spread much news some good some bad,
I've made people happy, made people sad.

I have been used in many ways,
From writing books to writing plays.
I've broken hearts and solved some crime,
I've been around from early time.

Without me life would be uninformed,
No reading 'round fires as feet are warmed.
No way to educate the masses
And gain advance as life it passes.

I've fought my corner, changed many a mind,
Help those in war their peace to find.
Proved many times home and abroad,
The pen is mightier than the sword.

The Last Oak Tree

The Oak Tree stood and muttered,
"When will humans ever learn?
They're destroying all the forests,
Destruction everywhere they turn"
He wistfully recalled memories,
Of golden times in days gone by,
When trees were left to flourish,
Growing strong and reaching high.

He looked around the forest,
Where more than one young tree had died,
His body shuddered mournfully,
And the once proud tree, he cried.
He remembered as a sapling,
Watching men ride off to war,
Collecting wood to make their weapons,
Returning many times for more.

He closed his eyes, let his mind travel,
Throughout the ravaged age of time,
Recalling all the devastation,
Caused for no reason or no rhyme.
Before then, the land was covered,
By swaying, dancing, whispering trees,
Young saplings' roots were growing,
And branches displayed their leaves.

The wind blew and orchestrated
These dancing leaves in joyful song.
Birds built nests high in their branches,
And, in harmony, sang along.
But over time man's thoughtless actions,
Have reduced the forest's size,
And now, where once a tree was living,
A rotten carcase lies.

No more will leaves be dancing,
No more, will proud trees sway,
Without a prick of conscience,
Lumberjacks just hack away.
If they could only hear the crying,
Shrieks of devastation and despair,
From the trees that they were killing,
Would they take some time to care?

Would they stop what they were doing?
Start giving nature their respect?
Is it too late to reconsider?
And their mistakes, can they correct?
Will man's insatiable need to conquer,
Destroying everything they see,
Blind their mind to consequences,
And how disastrous results will be?

No, they continue to turn land barren,
Happy when forests exist no more,
With no branches for the birds to nest in,
Or no teaming flora on the floor.
The birds have all moved onward
To build themselves another home,
Not knowing where they'll settle,
Each day, endlessly, they'll roam.

Wildlife has all been scattered,
Some are killed without remorse.
No thought for their survival,
While man pursues his deadly cause.
The oak tree knows his time is ending,
As the march of man destroys,
He can hear the humans getting closer,
You can't mistake their killing noise.

The years of his education,
Numerous sights and sounds absorbed,
Will each in turn be emptied,
From within the place they're stored.
The humans walk up to him,
They prepare for their first cut,
The blade quickly fires into action,
As the safety guard is shut.

One last glance around the forest,
As he hears the whirling sound,
The lumberjack shouts "Timber,"
And the oak tree hits the ground.
The last oak tree lies prostate,
No longer upright, proud and tall,
He's surrounded by the workers,
Who all watched his final fall.

Smiling and patting shoulders,
Workers put all their tools away,
Soon they will travel homeward,
They've killed enough tall trees today.
No other trees are standing,
Destroyed to satiate man's greed,
Men move forever onward,
Their lust for power and wealth to feed.

The oak tree, slowly dying,
Relinquishes memories he'd held,
As each one has started fading,
From the moment he was felled.
But over time, new life starts growing,
As the seeds of life are spread,
Then gradually and slowly,
Plants start rising from the dead.

The Unwanted Friend

"Stand quite still", the voice boomed loud.
The people quaked with fear.
They stood with eyes wide open.
Waiting for someone to appear.
The sky was clear and vacant,
No cloud was there to see.
Then the unseen voice again boomed out,
"I want to talk with thee".

The sound fills all the hollows,
It flows out of the walls,
It emanates out of the floor,
Where ever the sunlight falls.
The heads of all the people
Were slowly turning 'round.
To try to spot the origin,
Of this loud compelling sound.

"From this day forth I own you,
My will you must obey.
Your minds will react every time
You hear the words I say.
Don't search, you will not find me.
Ubiquitous I am.
"Your life I will extinguish,
Whether woman, child or man".

As if to prove his power,
Each person sixty on,
Closed their eyes, then gave a cry,
Fell down, their life force it was gone.
"But do not fear I'm really friendly,.
I'll not hurt the rest of you.
As long as you obey my voice
And do what I want you to.

The first thing is your army
Must allegiance to me swear,
Then throw away their uniforms,
I'll give them all new ones to wear.
All problems of society,
My police they'll handle well,
So if you see wrong-doing,
My police you must go tell.

The paper on the presses will,
Print only what is good
For you to know, & it will help
You live the way you should"
"Who owns this voice", the people asked,
"Why has it come in here?
It's made enough bold statements,
"They've come over loud and clear".

"Don't question me, don't wonder,
You've seen what I can do.
Now just go on about your deeds,
I'll be back to talk to you".
The people went on living,
New fear etched upon their face.
Each one searching out for solace,
But for them, there was no place.

If someone dared to question,
The voice and its' foul deeds.
Mysteriously they vanished,
Their punishment to receive.
Their families said "The police came
And took them fast away.
We've no idea where they have gone.
There is no more to say".

People worked and people toiled
To build a country closed.
A country free from influence
And the questions that they posed.
Their minds each day grew blanker.
Their power ebbed ever weak.
No longer thinking new thoughts,
And no new words they'd speak.

The voice some time went silent,
But its' works they still went on.
It persevered along its' course
Until resistance was all gone.
"I am their friend, it's for their good.
I know what's for the best.
But this is only one country,
Now I'll work on all the rest".

Who Cares?

The rain was falling down outside,
A battered baby inside cried.
Her mothers' sitting drinking gin.
No one hears the cry from deep within.
A face now battered black and blue,
What else is she allowed to do?
The baby has no food tonight.
For a living chance it has to fight.

A healthy child when it was born,
Brought joy to all that summer morn.
The family all sat 'round the bed,
Smiled and stared at the baby's head.
A lovely child, a mothers' pride,
Wanted since she was a bride.
Now her life's' ambition recognised,
Holds baby tight, so highly prized.

Then nights of sleep soon disappeared,
Disenchantment's doleful head, soon reared.
The pleasure of the birth now gone,
The pressures grow, can't carry on.
The cries continue, they pierce the air,
Oh, how she wished it was not there.
Her husband's had enough, leaves home
Takes to the street, decides to roam.

No peace at home, no happiness,
He feels his life is such a mess.
No room for what they had before,
Too young to care, can take no more.
Back at the home, she feels betrayed,
No answers to the prayers she'd prayed.
Its' not her fault, she's not to blame.
They were happy 'till the baby came.

There at the cots' side she looks down,
At the crying child, in dirty gown.
The noise goes on can take no more,
Soon the child is on the floor.
Her foot is lifted, and hard does land,
Breaking bones in a tiny hand.
But the punishment, does not end there,
Soon the child flies through the air.

It crashes hard against the wall,
And to the floor in pain does fall.
As babies blood spreads o'er the floor,
She leaves the room; she's closed the door.
A glass is knocked, the drink is spilt,
She needs a way, to cover guilt.
The bottle she takes to her lips,
Drinks quickly down, no time for sips.

Now there she sits drunk in the chair,
No need to know, she does not care.
Neighbours ignore the babies' cries,
They could help, but no one tries.
Behind closed doors they close their mind
Not caring what the morn will find,
Soon pills and drink, prove what's been said,
Silence falls; they're both now dead.

The Demon

"You'll burn in hell", the spirit said,
To the people cowering down.
In the corner of the room they were,
And their screaming he did drown.

His fingers travelled 'round the room,
Pointing to each one in turn,
They all thought they knew it all,
But there was much they had to learn.

"I'll teach you all you shouldn't dabble,
You came in here an arrogant race,
Now you're a crying mumbling group,
I see such fear in every face".

They all were quite amiable,
When first they came together,
Their talk it jumped through subjects,
Ranging from football and the weather.

Then one voice said, "We've thirteen here,
A seance let us hold,
We'll see what it is all about",
Then cards he began to cut and fold.

A letter he put on each card,
From A right down to Z,
We'll use the tumbler over there,
To make contact with the dead".

With lights made dim, they gathered 'round,
On the table cards spread out,
They were all prepared to have a laugh,
Of that there was no doubt.

"Place your fingers up on the glass,
Be silent, do not push",
While he tried to call a spirit up,
In the room there was a hush.

"Oh, spirit of the time gone by,
Appear to us, we want to talk".
Nothing happened for a while,
Then he turned as white as chalk.

The others gasped and looked at him,
Fingers still pressing on the glass,
Then from one letter to another,
It slowly began to pass.

It read, "A spirit soon will come,
An answer to your request,
It will appear as per your demand,
I'm sure you'll like your guest.

The glass it stopped, their faces grim,
No one dared make a sound.
Then a puff of smoke and a flash of light,
Rose up out of the ground.

A piercing screech and a deafening howl,
Attacked each and every ear,
Then a form unique and hideous,
Above the table did appear.

Trying to escape our thirteen friends,
All rushed towards the door,
But before they made their exit,
Flames sprouted from the floor.

Shouts rang out, when they saw the form,
And beheld its unseemly face,
"I thank you one and all my friends,
For allowing me, into your place".

A wicked snarl, and evil eyes,
An ugliness they'd never seen,
Emitted from its every pore,
So unwelcome and unclean.

Now our thirteen friends are cowering down,
Faces covered by their hands.
Then slowly, out of their control,
They each began to stand.

"You may have thought you'd have some fun,
And call me from my rest.
But now you'll face the consequence,
Of putting spirits to the test.

Each one here you silly fools,
Have ended life on earth,
The flames you see before you here,
Await to grant you your new birth.

You'll find that it's not pleasant,
It's a place that's filled with pain,
And when my work up here is done,
I'll return down there again.

And you'll be coming with me,
My pleasure, not yours, I fear,
So enjoy your last few moments,
Your time is very near".

They tried to find a hiding place,
They were trapped, their future dire,
Then a bible they saw across the room,
Unburnt amidst the fire.

"Let's try to reach across the room,
And receive from it protection.
Then as one body they did run,
All in the same direction.

Hands full of sweat, grabbed at the book,
They felt safe when they were there.
Then the host of the house they'd entered,
"Please help us", he said in prayer.

Then in unison psalm 23,
From each quivering mouth sang out,
They asked God if in his mercy,
If their situation he'd turnabout.

Then all at once, the room it spun,
It seemed flames were everywhere.
There was shouting, and screaming and unearthly sounds,
Filling each molecule of the air.

The spirit ranted, rolled in and out
Of the flames it brought into existence,
And although he tried to put up a fight,
It was a weak resistance.

Then all at once, a lightening flash,
A howling wind and almighty roar,
When our thirteen friends next opened their eyes,
The spirit, it was no more.

They fell onto their knees and offered a prayer,
Thanking God for his saving act,
They asked the Lord for wisdom,
It was something they knew they all lacked.

They ripped up the cards and shattered the glass,
Clearing the mess there where they had been,
Determined there'd be no repeating,
Of that unearthly, frightening scene.

The Christmas Party

It was our works Christmas party,
And we were gathered by the bar.
Drinks paid for by our bosses,
Who had arrived in a chauffeured car.
I was standing with my workmates,
While we all surveyed the room,
Then I saw a walking goddess,
She made my heart go BOOM!

Her eyes were so appealing,
Hair which shimmered in the light.
The body of a goddess,
For which I'd gladly fight.
Boys' were staring, following, watching,
As she floated across the floor.
Then she smiled as she went by me,
It was then I wanted more.

She was alone, without her boyfriend,
There was no one for me to fear.
So, I took hold of my lager,
And I sidled very near.
She looked up as I approached her,
And when I asked her for a dance
She smiled and looked me over,
How I prayed she take a chance.

Reaching for her hand to guide her,
Through the throbbing sweating mass,
She stopped and kissed my fingers,
It was then I dropped my glass.
As we danced, our bodies moulded.
With each beat our hearts entwined,
Would she have danced so closely?
Knowing what I had in mind.

After drinks, we danced together,
All night long we moved as one.
I was sure we'd go on dancing,
When the music had all gone.
We danced slow, I held her tightly,
Then softly whispered in her ear,
"Would you like a ride in my car,
To a place I know quite near?"

She looked at me, with both eyes twinkling,
Gave a smile and bowed her head,
It was then I thought I'd blown it,
But she kissed my cheek instead.
She asked me where my car was,
I gently pulled her by her hand.
And I led her to the car park,
Waving "Goodbye", to the band.

As we drove her head was resting
On my shoulder, oh what joy.
She stretched up and kissed my ear lobe,
And with my hair began to toy.
How I hurried to seclusion,
Far away from prying eyes,
Where my dreams would all be answered,
And I'd hopefully win first prize.

When we stopped, she quickly clambered
Onto the long seat in the rear.
With her hand she seductively called me,
Making her meaning very clear.
It was my Birthday...it was Christmas.
My best days rolled into one.
Any doubts about her shyness
From that moment, were all gone.

Lying on the back seat with her,
I kissed her gently on the lips.
Then my hands gently began exploring,
Her soft hair, her shapely hips.
We took turns to "pop" the buttons
On her blouse then on my shirt.
As I turned, I caught my ankle,
Unaware of how much it hurt.

She slid off her blouse and lay there,
As I fumbled with her bra,
It was then that I got the feeling,
We weren't alone inside the car.
I turned around...I saw her father.
He'd come to find his little girl.
I muttered words of nonsense,
As my head began to whirl.

I said we were only playing,
A silly game, no more than that...
We were talking of our hobbies,
I tried but my words fell flat.
He reached into the car and grabbed me.
Then he dragged me through the door,
Punched my face and sent me crashing,
I fell hard upon the floor.

She screamed and said I'd forced her,
In the club I'd spiked her drink,
And when her glass was empty,
She'd been confused, she could not think.
Then she told a sordid story,
Of how I'd stripped her in the car,
And how glad she was to see him,
Before I'd gone too far.

His face flushed bright red with anger
And he pulled hard at my hair.
I shouted my objections,
When my scalp began to tear.
He stopped and started sneering,
And said he'd had a good idea.
He then relieved me of my trousers.
Making his intentions very clear.

They drove off, leaving me naked,
Freezing cold inside the park,
Turning white just like a snowman,
All surrounded by the dark.
Suddenly a dog was barking,
Breaking the stillness of the night.
I quickly began to search for shelter,
As I realised my plight.

But too late, its owner saw me,
I was nearly deafened by her scream.
I tried explaining my situation,
Saying "Things are not as they first seem".
She stared...she closed her eyes...then fainted,
Falling in a crumpled heap.
And as I rushed to give her comfort,
From the bushes, men did leap.

One man grabbed my arms, and held me.
Shouting "Someone fetch the police.
We can't have drunken perverts,
Disturbing honest peoples' peace".
I crouched down, I felt embarrassed,
To hide my modesty, I tried.
I knew no-one there would listen,
I just bowed my head and cried.

My night at the Christmas party,
A few friendly drinks with friends.
Turned into a night of no forgetting,
And one that seemingly won't end.
Sitting wrapped up in a blanket,
Worrying about my friends and folks,
Knowing from this moment onwards,
I'll be the ultimate of Christmas jokes.

Wheel

At ten to two some hold me,
Some like a quarter before three,
They long to get me in their fingers,
When my comely form they see.

Their fingers mould around me
They let them move and gently slide.
Their caress is so appealing
As we commence our little ride.

There are those who hold with one hand,
The other searching for things to do.
Doing things they know they shouldn't.
I much prefer being held by two.

Sometimes they treat me like a plaything,
Like an object, a thing of fun.
When they tap me with their fingers,
Or they beat me like a drum.

To others I'm just a guitar,
They strum their fingers, frame their chords.
Some they play me like their organ,
Music brings its' own rewards.

But no matter how they treat me,
I know they'll never go too far.
They need to touch and hold me gently.
When they want to steer their car.

Did God Forget?

I woke up on Tuesday morning,
The sky was dull and grey.
There was no sound of singing,
All the birds had flown away.
I tried but found no people,
Not one person was around.
I strained eyes and strained my ears,
But I could not hear a sound.

My house was lying empty,
My wife had left, no-one next door.
I ran until I exhausted,
Then fell panting to the floor.
The sweat was running freely,
My clothes they were soaking wet.
There was nobody left on Earth,
Could it be, did God forget?

Am I the only person living,
Where has everybody gone?
Two people last night were in bed,
This morning just the one.
I don't know what to do now,
I keep running around,
I see no people walking,
No shadows on the ground.

No airplanes are flying,
The sky is very clear,
I want to see somebody,
A sound I want to hear.
I'm really very scared now,
I'm starting now to fret,
Why am I all alone on earth?
Could it be, did God forget?

I'm running, calling, crying,
My heart is full of fear,
No matter where I'm looking,
I can find nobody here.
No birds can I see flying,
No cats or dogs I see,
Each living thing has vanished,
The last one on earth is me.

What's that? A light is shining,
It is growing very clear,
Above my thoughts of panic,
A distant voice I hear.
The voice I hear is calming,
No hidden hint of threat,
I feel now deep down in my heart,
My God did not forget.

My name the voice is calling,
So gentle and serene,
I see a soothing colour,
It is a gentle shade of green.
I try to give an answer,
But my mouth I cannot move,
Then as the light gets clearer,
My movements do improve.

A nurse is standing near me,
A warm smile is on her face.
Then I remember where I am now,
I recognise this place.
I've had an operation,
And for that I'm in their debt,
But they can't dispel the feeling,
When I thought God did forget.

The scenes were all imagined,
Although to me so very real,
I can remember all the stresses
The disturbing horror I still feel.
All my fears are irrational,
And I'm covered now in sweat.
As I relive the bad experience,
When I thought God did forget.

Release Your Mind

Close your eyes, open your mind
Just let your spirit drift.
Leave your body on the floor,
And your inner conscience lift.
Think of the places in the world,
To where you'd like to go.
Be it on a mountain high,
Or in a valley low.
See yourself in fields of green,
Or flying like a bird,
Climbing high above the clouds,
Or floating on a word.
Leave this world of trouble,
And your enemies far behind,
The trials and stress of modern life,
Sweet tranquillity go find.
Yes, float around in happiness,
With love yourself surround,
Have no tears or grieving there,
Let peace and joy abound.

Be Free

A disguised voice in my mind,
Is appealing to me,
To go out, seek, search and find,
A place where I'm free.
It's tired of being locked up,
It's tired of standards here.
It's tired of others sipping its' cup,
And it just wants to make it clear.

This disguised voice in my mind
That's appealing to me,
To be like the migrating bird,
And taking off across the sea.
It's tired of being locked up,
It's tired of standards here.
It just wants to take off right now,
And from the rat race disappear.

My Time to Die.

Who can it be?
Who gave them the right?
To make my short day,
Into a long, long night.
I made a mistake,
I took someone's life,
I was guilty I know,
Now I'm living in strife.
At least him I killed
He did not know,
When he was to die,
Goodbye, I must go.

Butterfly

The butterfly won’t talk or sing,
Just flies around all day,
It flutters by you as you watch,
And then goes on its' way.

Red Mini Boat

The little red mini boat
Across the sea did roll,
Making such an awful din,
Enough to frighten every soul.
Then one day someone got annoyed,
Put bricks into its' tank,
The next time it tried to cross the sea,
The poor little boat, it sank.

Plastic Coated Biscuit

The plastic-coated biscuit,
Was a trick to be enjoyed.
Little Johnny bought it,
And with everyone he toyed.
It was tried on aunty Mary,
And uncle Charlie too.
If you are not careful,
It will be tried on you.

The Bear

I once knew people who went to find,
A big forest bear who was nice and kind,
They went to his cave, knocked over his cup,
Then the bear got angry and ate them all up.

I once knew a bear who was stung by a bee,
It jumped so high right over a tree.
He went up so high, and travelled so far,
When he came down, he squashed the rangers' car.

I once knew a bear that thought he could sing,
Thought he could make the cowbells ring.
But he opened his mouth and no noise came out.
A frog laughed as he passed, the bear gave him a clout.

I once knew a bear who was always wild,
But he fell in love, became meek and mild.
He was so very shy, didn't know what to do,
His new love left him, now he's feeling blue.

I once knew a bear who bought a car,
But he could not drive, so he did not go far.
His hat fell over his eyes, he just could not see,
So he crashed through a gate, and ran into a tree.

I once knew a bear whose teeth did ache,
When he took a bite of a chocolate cake.
Then with his both hands, his mouth he did cup,
And a snake pinched the cake, and then ate it all up.

I once knew a bear who fell fast asleep,
When into his cave, a wolf did creep.
Then the bear breathed deep sucked in all the air
When I looked for the wolf, he was not there.

I once knew a bear who lived in a cave,
He was kind and gentle, so well behaved.
'Till he took a drink, and it went to his head,
They went 'round and shot him, and now he's dead.

Thank you, I hope you have enjoyed your journey.

Printed in Poland
by Amazon Fulfillment
Poland Sp. z o.o., Wrocław

60143685R00089